Tulips and Treason

Tulips and Treason

Tristi Pinkston

WALNUT SPRINGS PRESS

For the one who almost was.

Walnut Springs Press
110 South 800 West
Brigham City, Utah 84302
http://walnutspringspress.blogspot.com

ISBN: 978-1-59992-900-2

Other Mysteries by Tristi Pinkston

Secret Sisters

Dearly Departed

Hang 'Em High

Targets in Ties

Till Death Do Us Part

ACKNOWLEDGMENTS

As always and forever will be, my first thanks go to my husband, Matt. He never gets any less awesome or supportive. Thanks for everything you do, honey! I also want to say thanks to my great kids—Caryn, Ammon, Joseph, and Benjamin. You guys are my world.

My critique group is an invaluable resource to me. Keith, Kim, Heather, and Nichole—you rock. A big thanks too to our new members—Jaclyn, Steve, and Jessica. Your input makes my stories so much better, and your friendship makes my life so much happier.

Special thanks to John and Danyelle Ferguson. John, you've finally gotten your wish and been killed in a book. I hope it wasn't too painful. I tried to make it quick.

Congratulations to contest winners Karlene, Jill, and Betty—you'll find the names you chose inside.

And last, but definitely not least, I'd like to thank Ida Mae, Tansy, and Arlette for making another appearance. They may not be the main characters this time around, but they will always be the stars of the show.

ONE

Antonio ducked behind a red-brick building. His feet landed in a puddle formed by rainwater dripping off the roof and splashing onto the ground of the alleyway. He held his breath, listening for the sound of a car driving by and watching for the flash of headlights, knowing it was only a matter of time before the white stretch limo passed his hiding spot. All was quiet. Everyone had gone to bed hours before, and the streets echoed faintly with the bark of a dog or the whistle of a breeze, but that was all.

He squeezed his eyes shut, wishing he'd listened to his mother years ago when she'd warned him about getting involved with Scarlotti. "He's up to no good, Tony," she told him, piling his plate high with her famous spaghetti and marinara sauce. She believed the way to his ears was through his stomach, and she would've been right if not for the fact that he was greedy. He wanted the things Scarlotti offered, but now, a decade later, Antonio was paying the price.

After hiding in the dark alley for fifteen minutes, he cautiously poked his head around the corner, wondering if by some miracle he'd given Scarlotti's men the slip. He saw nothing, and heard nothing but the drip of water from the roof. Maybe he was safe.

"I wouldn't go out there if I were you, Tony." The deep voice behind him was full of amusement. "Someone might be looking for you."

Antonio turned slowly and faced the muzzle of a semi-automatic pistol. Fear grabbed his throat, nearly making him choke. "Hi, Damien," he said, spreading his hands wide in an exaggerated shrug. "How's it going?"

"Very well, now that I've got what I came for." Damien Scarlotti grabbed Tony's arm, spun him around, and pushed him face-first onto the pavement. Tony felt the impact as a bullet entered his back, and then everything faded away.

Jack and Molly sat in the waiting room outside Special Agent Blevins' office, nerves tight, jaws clenched. Molly toyed with the lid of her Starbucks cup until the rim cracked. Then she finished the drink in a series of gulps and threw the cup into the trash can on the other side of a ficus tree.

"You're not going to tell him, are you?" She leaned back on the leather sofa. "I mean, I don't think I'm ready for that."

"I'm not going to tell him."

Molly looked at her husband—really looked at him like she hadn't for the last three days. His dark hair lay in waves against his head in a casual "I'm too good-looking to know how good-looking I am" sort of way. His eyes, usually bright, were clouded. They were what first drew her in back when they were assigned to be partners. She hadn't meant to fall in love with him, but his eyes wouldn't take no for an answer.

"At least he's the only one who knows," Jack continued. "It would be harder if we had to tell everyone."

FBI agents weren't supposed to fall in love with each other, and they most definitely weren't supposed to get married. Jack Coleman and Molly North had broken some pretty hefty rules when they stepped into a wedding chapel while on assignment in Mexico. They'd told Agent Blevins, fearing he would have them thrown out of the agency, but he'd supported them in keeping their marriage a secret, not wanting to lose them.

Molly sighed, thinking about the fight she and Jack had the other night and the decision they'd made to divorce after five very happy years and four very miserable months. Maybe the FBI had more reasons than one for their policy prohibiting agents from marrying each other.

Ashley, Agent Blevins' long-legged secretary in four-inch stilettos, exited his office and held the door open. "Agent Coleman, Agent North, please come in." Jack stood, pulled his suit jacket straight, and headed for the office. Molly was right behind. Once upon a time, she'd wished she could take his last name, but now it was all for the best. It would be too hard to change it back after the divorce.

Agent Blevins sat behind his desk, imposing as ever. "Thank you for coming in on such short notice this morning. I have something extremely important to tell you."

"What's going on?" Molly took the seat Jack held for her. He'd always done that, from the time they were first assigned to each other.

Agent Blevins leaned forward and steepled his fingers, resting his elbows on the desk. He waited to speak until Ashley brought in coffee, served it, and then left as quietly as she'd come in. "We have a break in the Scarlotti investigation, and I'm putting you two on it."

"What?" Jack sat up straight, his spine rigid. Only the stars of the agency had been put on that case. Molly knew he'd been watching it with envy for the last couple of years, but his chance just hadn't come. He had frequently shared with her his frustration at being excluded from the task force, and she figured his brain was exploding right now.

"That's right. We had a call from the feds in Salt Lake City. Seems one of Scarlotti's former henchmen decided to turn informant."

"And he's still alive?"

"Barely." Agent Blevins flipped open a folder and pulled out an 8 x 10 glossy photo. The background was a little grainy, but the face that looked back from the page was clear. Molly felt pulled toward him. Blevins went on, "This young man, Antonio Maglione, was shot in the back by Scarlotti at point-blank range and survived. He was found by someone in the sheriff's department in a small Utah town and transported to Salt Lake for treatment. He spilled his guts to the police, who called the Salt Lake feds, who called us. We spread the story that the kid died at the hospital, and with any luck, Scarlotti believes it."

"Where is Antonio now?" Jack asked.

"He was released from the hospital and is downstairs resting. And telling us everything he knows." Blevins waved the picture, which caught a current of air and wafted back and forth. "He's the break we've been waiting for."

Jack's hands balled into fists and then relaxed. Molly could tell he was trying to stay calm and professional, but she had no doubt that once they left the office, he'd have plenty to say. "What's our next move?" he asked Blevins.

"I've been on the horn all morning with the higher-ups, gathering what intel I could. Turns out they've been keeping an eye on Utah for a while, but for different reasons. They've traced several instances of money laundering and drug trafficking to an area in the northern part of the state. Now we know that our cases overlap. This brings me to you." Agent Blevins flicked his eyes back and forth between Molly and Jack. "I'm sending you undercover."

Her heart began to pound. She loved going undercover. "Tell us more, sir."

Blevins stood and walked over to a large whiteboard in the corner of his office. Jack and Molly swiveled in their chairs to get a better view as Blevins pulled a series of photos from a large envelope and attached them to the board with magnets. "Antonio, our shooting-victim-turned-informant, works for Scarlotti." Blevins pointed to the pictures as he spoke.

Scarlotti was kind of handsome, Molly decided, if you liked that scary, arrogant look in a guy. She took a sip from her cup, wondering what Ashley had done to ruin the coffee this time. It took a special kind of talent to do what she did.

"Scarlotti's rival is a man named Fabiano." Blevins pointed to a third picture. Fabiano, an older man with beefy jowls, looked nothing like the romance cover model Fabio, even if their names were similar. However, Fabiano had a certain charm about him—it was something in his eyes, Molly decided. They looked friendly, almost twinkly. "Fabiano has been operating out of Utah for some time, but the Salt Lake feds haven't closed in on him yet. Nothing we have so far would stand up in court. But then he contacted Scarlotti about making a deal. He wants to meet Scarlotti and talk about merging the two organizations. Scarlotti's had men in Utah for a while as well and they've bumped into Fabiano's men from time to time, but the two dons have never met. This is going to give us the opportunity we need."

"How do we come into all this, sir?" Jack asked.

"Fate has smiled upon us kindly." Blevins crossed the room and handed another picture to Jack. "This is the man who goes by the name Joe Baker. He's Scarlotti's cousin-in-law, and he's pretty big in the organization. Thanks to Antonio, we apprehended Baker last night and have him under tight security. Joe is supposed to be the go-between for the two organizations until Scarlotti decides if he can trust Fabiano, and vice versa. And now that we have Baker, we have the key to bringing this whole thing down."

Molly peered over Jack's shoulder. Joe Baker stared at

her from the photo, his dark hair and blue eyes giving him a kind of Remington Steele look.

"You have the same coloring and are roughly the same height as Joe Baker," Agent Blevins told Jack. "Your assignment is to impersonate him, contact Fabiano, assure him of Scarlotti's good intentions, and set up a meeting between the two. You will then gather whatever evidence you can on both organizations and help us shut them down together."

Molly felt a tingle race down her arms. "Wow."

"Wow is right, Molly. This is quite the opportunity."

Jack studied the picture a moment longer. "Sounds good, sir. When do we start?"

"Immediately. The trick is going to be establishing your cover. This exchange of information isn't a one-time deal. Scarlotti wants to feel out Fabiano very carefully, so you'll probably interact with the man four or five times before you ever set up the meeting between the two dons."

"And our cover?" Molly asked.

"This is where things get a little tricky. To Fabiano, you, Jack, are Joe Baker. He's expecting you to come to town, purchase a small business, and run it with your female associate to give the impression of down-home respectability. Your names will be Jason and Sarah Bennett. We have purchased a floral shop, which is now undergoing renovations to become an ultimate command center. You will run the shop by day and bring down the mob by night."

"Wait," Jack said. "Won't Scarlotti know I'm not Joe Baker? I mean, they're related and all."

Agent Blevins sighed. "It does present an additional complication. You'll have to be very careful in how you relay information back to Scarlotti. They do most of their communicating by burner phone and rarely meet face-to-face, so you should be able to avoid seeing him for the time being. Baker's voice is always muffled by a voice changer, so that will be helpful."

"He muffles his voice to talk to his own cousin-in-law?" Molly asked. "Seems a little odd to me."

"Baker takes extra precautions for his own safety and that of the organization. There's too much at stake."

Molly nodded. "So, about this 'female associate' thing. What does she do?"

"Well, she arranges the flowers, of course."

Molly blinked. "But isn't that kind of sexist? I mean, men can arrange flowers, can't they?"

Agent Blevins looked at her pointedly. "What's the matter, Molly?"

"It's just . . ." She squirmed a little in her seat. She'd never balked at an assignment before and didn't want to come across wrong. "I'm not in the least bit creative, Agent Blevins. You know me—I'm a weapons girl. I'm out on the range, blasting away at targets. I don't make things. I don't paint or crochet . . . I don't even cook. I mean, I really, *really* don't cook. Couldn't we run a gun shop instead?"

Agent Blevins frowned. "I'm sorry, Molly. We have to move quickly, and this floral shop is the only business in town that is already established, in good condition, and up for sale. We don't have time to wait until the store of your choice presents itself. And yes, I suppose men do arrange flowers, but Joe Baker doesn't. He's part of a Mafia family and a very trusted employee of a high-powered don. Playing with roses is not something he would do—that's why he has an assistant to do it for him."

Molly sighed. She didn't want to let her lack of domesticity get in the way. "All right, sir. I'll do my best." Something occurred to her. "You said you have the real Joe Baker in custody. What about his real associate? She's not going to show up and blow the whistle, is she?"

"She left town as soon as we picked Joe up, and we've got men looking for her now. She's running scared. I don't think she'll cause any problems, but we won't dismiss the possibility."

"That's good to know, sir."

"Now for the assignment. Do you know anything about floral arranging?"

"I know what flowers are." Molly thought it was a good place to start. "Beyond that, no."

"I've brought in the wife of one of our agents to help you. She's a floral designer—has her own shop and everything—and she'll show you the ropes."

"You mean I can't just look it up on YouTube or something?"

"Sorry, this is a very hands-on type of career."

Molly slouched a little and then realized it didn't look very professional or agent-like, so she sat upright again.

"Now," Agent Blevins said, slapping a book on the desk, "I need you to choose your color scheme."

"Color scheme?" Molly could shoot a gun with unerring accuracy. She could throw a three-hundred-pound crook on the floor and cuff him, and she could disable a bomb—all without breaking a sweat. But suddenly she felt very overwhelmed.

"For the shop."

She opened the book, which turned out to be some kind of sample portfolio for interior decorating. All the layouts looked fine to her. In fact, to her undiscriminating eye, they all looked exactly the same. She pointed. "This one?"

"Great." Agent Blevins pressed a button. Ashley came in and he handed her the book. "Call Utah and tell them she picked page four."

"Very good, sir. I would have chosen that one as well, Molly—plum and sage are very restful colors." Ashley filled Molly's cup from a decanter she held in her other hand, then strode out of the office. Molly appreciated the secretary's attention to her caffeine habit, but today's blend strongly resembled brown water with one little coffee particle floating on top. And what was up with "plum" and "sage"? Looked purple and green to her.

Agent Blevins resumed speaking to Jack and Molly. "One more thing. Utah has a Mormon population of sixty-two percent, and the town where you'll be going is eighty-nine percent. We think you'll fit in a lot better if you pose as Mormons."

Molly leaned forward. "Excuse me, sir—did you say you wanted us to be morons?"

Agent Blevins' mouth twitched. "No, I said Mormons. They are a religious faction. You'll need to bone up on their beliefs, but essentially their faith revolves around their assertion that some angels appeared to a teenager and gave him a gold book. They also like naming their towns after people found in that book."

"Um . . . are you *sure* you didn't say morons, sir?"

"It does sound unusual, I know, but these people are very staunch in their faith, and you'll need to pretend to believe as they do. Ashley will give you a packet of study material."

Agent Blevins rose from his desk. "We have a lot to do. Prepare to be gone indefinitely. I want you back here tomorrow morning at six o'clock sharp, ready to learn the ins and outs of floral design. You'll also have a chance to meet up with Antonio and hear his story from his own mouth. We'll ship you out to Utah on Friday, but you'll be bunking here in the meantime. Your training will be nearly round-the-clock."

"And just where exactly are we going, sir?" Molly asked.

"To a little place high in the mountains—a town called Omni."

TWO

Molly stood in her walk-in closet, hands on her hips, studying the clothes that hung from the rod. "I don't have any long dresses," she said. "And I definitely don't have any bonnets or pinafores."

"What are you talking about?" Jack sat on the edge of the bed. "Why would you need a bonnet? And what's a pinafore?"

"You know, one of those apron thingies Amish people wear." Molly rested her forearm on the closet doorjamb. "I may need to go shopping. Is there a Mormon clothes store somewhere around here? Do they even have Mormons in L.A.?"

"I don't think it's going to be that hard." Jack picked up a magazine from the information packet Ashley had given them, which Molly had dumped all over the bed. "Look. These people are wearing normal clothes." He pointed at the picture on the cover.

"The *Ensign*? What, are we on *Star Trek* now?" Molly held out her hand. "Can I see that?" Flipping through the pages, she saw women in dresses, women in skirts . . . Ah, there was a woman in pants, and no bonnets anywhere. What a relief. "So it looks like I just need to wear conservative clothes. I can do that."

"And take a lot of dresses. I get the feeling we're going to do a bunch of churchy stuff."

Molly felt sorry for Jack. He wasn't the most religiously inclined guy in the world. He had really good intuition and often sensed things while they were out in the field, but he laughed off any talk of spiritualism or mysticism. He chalked up everything to instinct, and for the most part, Molly agreed with him. She just didn't see much point in going to church and singing songs while waving her arms in the air, like she'd seen on TV. She imagined she and Jack would both get their fill of it long before this assignment was over.

She went back into the closet, feeling more confident now. She pulled out shirts, blouses, slacks, and jeans for the Mormon part of her assignment, and then grabbed some of her flashier clothing for her role as Joe Baker's assistant. After much internal debating, Molly left behind her leopard-print miniskirt.

"So, are you going to pack?" she asked Jack. "I'm almost done with my clothes, and you haven't even started."

"Yeah, I'd better go." He stood and stretched. "I'll see ya later."

"Do you . . ." She hesitated. "Do you want to come back over in a little while and share a pizza?"

He met her eyes, blue touching brown. "I'd like that." Then he was gone, walking into the garage to slip through the passageway they'd built between his place and hers.

Keeping their marriage a secret had been difficult, but in some ways, it had also been fun. They found and purchased two condos side by side and decorated them according to their own tastes, his very much a bachelor pad, and hers—well, hers not much better, to be honest. She did have a few more pictures on the walls, but that was as far as she'd taken it. Then they built the passageway between so they could still be together without anyone knowing.

Their neighbors had tried to set Jack up with their daughters or nieces, but he used work as his excuse for not dating. Molly had been told by one well-meaning octogenarian that she was in her prime—anything younger than thirty-five was highly desirable, apparently—and she should start going to mixers to find a man. Molly had no idea what a mixer even was. Sounded like a martini.

With all the would-be matchmakers working on Jack's love life as well as hers, for some reason no one had tried to set them up with each other. Molly wondered if their neighbors knew how incompatible they were. She wished she'd had that insight herself a long time ago. It would have saved her the heartache she was feeling now.

She finished filling up her suitcases and then walked around, studying her house. What else should she bring? Who knew how long they'd be gone. They'd be going straight from the California office to Omni, so anything she wanted, she had to grab now. She tucked a picture of her parents, whom she hardly ever got to see, into the side pocket of her small bag. Anything she needed but had forgotten, she could buy later. What she couldn't buy was a happy marriage.

Jack and Molly arrived at FBI headquarters right on time the next morning. Two agents took over the unloading of their car as they headed in to meet with Special Agent Blevins and Braden King, with whom they'd worked on other cases. A third man sat in the corner, slumped over a table, looking pale.

"Jack, Molly, this is Antonio Maglione, our informant in the Scarlotti case." Agent Blevins stepped to the side, and Jack and Molly walked over to the table. She could hardly contain her excitement. They were so close to seeing Scarlotti behind bars.

"Hi, Antonio." Jack reached out to shake his hand.

"Please, call me Tony."

"Tony, then. Thank you for coming in. I'm sure it wasn't easy. You know we want to make sure justice is served, right?"

Tony raised his head and offered a weak smile. "Yeah, I know, and I should have turned myself in a long time ago. But it was hard. They know where my mama lives. They know stuff . . ."

Molly touched his shoulder. She imagined he was pretty close to her age, but the way he sat, he looked like a scared little boy.

"The FBI is watching your mother right now, Tony, and we're going to do everything we can to help both of you," Agent Blevins said. "But you've got to keep trusting us, okay?"

Tony let out a deep breath. "That's why I'm here."

Molly and Jack sat on folding chairs near the table, and Agent Blevins handed each of them a folder. "Here's where we are right now. Fabiano isn't working out of Omni itself—he's got another hideout somewhere in the area. No one knows where it is but his top men. That will be one of your jobs, Jack. Get him to trust you and show you his fortress. He comes to Omni to meet with his other men and to arrange pickup and delivery of various goods. He also has rendezvous points in Orem, Provo, Spanish Fork . . ." At Molly's look of confusion, the agent paused. "Other towns in Utah. I'm providing you with a map so you can become generally familiar with the area. For some reason, Omni is where he chose to meet with Scarlotti's man, Joe Baker."

"How long has the agency been tracking Fabiano?" Jack asked.

"He's been on our radar for months, but we didn't realize he had a connection to Scarlotti until Tony here told us about him."

"Why did the mob choose Utah?" Molly asked. "It just seems so . . . quiet and boring."

Blevins nodded. "That's exactly why. Can't think of a place you'd be less likely to find the Mafia."

"But they'd also stick out. Blending in would be really difficult."

"Not as hard as you might think. People in Utah like wearing dark suits. They do it at least once a week, sometimes twice."

"Tell me more about Joe Baker," Jack said, opening his folder.

"He's the kind of man who keeps to himself. Remember, I told you he communicates by telephone—Scarlotti only sees him in person about once a year. Tony handled payment for services rendered. I'd say that Tony knows Joe Baker better than anyone, and Tony's on our side now."

"And what is Joe Baker's role in Scarlotti's organization?" Jack asked.

"He's Scarlotti's hit man," Tony replied.

"Hit man?" Molly raised an eyebrow. "That could get interesting."

"You know I'm up for the challenge, Molly." For some reason, Jack sounded a little offended, as if he thought she was questioning his ability to do his job. That was the furthest thing from her mind.

"I never said you weren't up for it," she hissed out of the corner of her mouth. Now was not the time for this type of discussion.

Agent Blevins glanced back and forth between them. "Now, there's just one more thing we need to do in regards to your cover, Jack."

"What's that?"

Braden King had been leaning against the wall during this conversation, but now he walked over and joined them in the center of the room. He was one of Molly's favorite agents to work with. He was a solid six-foot wall of muscle with sandy hair and brown eyes, and none of the other agents in the office had ever been able to best him in a practice spar. In contrast to this, though, was his sense of humor. He made everything fun, and Molly knew that if he was on the case, they'd have some good times.

"Baker has a gold tooth. It's very distinctive, and it's how his contacts identify him," Agent Blevins said.

"So that's why Braden's here?" Molly asked. Braden was trained in many different areas, but disguises were one of his specialties.

"Yes." Braden set his briefcase on a table in the corner of the room. "I'm going to do a little dentistry."

Molly shuddered. She'd once dug a bullet out of her own arm, but if there was anything in the world she couldn't stand, it was dental work—the whirring of the drill, especially. Oh, and having sharp things in her mouth. And the taste of rubber gloves. And . . .

"This will be no big deal." Braden held up a molded piece of gold. "I'll affix this to the tooth with strong dental adhesive. It will look like an actual gold tooth, and at the end of the assignment, it should come out fairly easily."

"You're going to glue it in his mouth?" Just the thought gave Molly the willies.

"It's all right," Jack said to her. "It's not like he's going to give me a scar or something."

Braden handed the piece of gold to Tony, who turned it over and nodded. "Yes, this looks right."

"Aren't all gold teeth the same?" Molly asked.

"Not Joe's." Braden passed it along to her, and she caught sight of the initials J.B. engraved on the outer surface.

"That's why we're the Bennetts," Molly said, "so Jack's initials will be the same and no one will ask him about the tooth."

"Exactly," Agent Blevins said.

"Ready, Jack?" Braden asked.

"Sure, go for it."

Braden placed a drape over Jack's chest and then pulled various implements out of his case. Molly cringed, her last root canal flashing before her eyes.

"I need to smooth down this area of your tooth," Braden explained. "Don't worry—I used to work for a dentist." He winked, and Molly didn't know if he was teasing or if he was trying to put her at ease. It had the opposite effect.

The sharp whir of a drill filled the air. "Wait! Aren't you going to numb him first?"

"Molly, I'm working with the surface of the tooth, where there are no nerves. If we needed to go any deeper, we wouldn't be doing it here—I'd take him to an actual medical facility. It's all right. Pretend like I'm just polishing it—that's essentially what I'm doing anyway."

Braden waited until she nodded and then brought the drill closer to Jack. Molly couldn't watch anymore—she turned away and tried not to shudder as the drill did its job.

"Man, that looks good," Braden said after several long minutes that were probably only long to Molly. "Tony, come check this out."

He braced his hands on the table and pushed himself up. "That does look good," he said, studying Jack from either side. Molly caught a flash of gold from one of Jack's incisors when he smiled.

"But will it stay in?" she asked. "We wouldn't want it popping off in the middle of dinner or anything."

"Molly, I'm hurt." Braden put a hand over his heart. "I'm a master."

Agent Blevins clapped Braden on the back, and the young agent left after gathering his supplies. Molly thought she might be sick. "How do you feel, Jack?" she asked.

"I'm fine. It's just a tooth." He turned back to Tony and began asking him questions about the relationship between Scarlotti and Joe Baker, both as cousins and businessmen. Molly didn't like the way Jack had just ignored her, but again, now was not the time to get into it. Maybe later, when they weren't in an important meeting with their boss and a key witness and getting ready to crack a huge case. Yeah, after that.

THREE

After leaving Tony, Jack and Molly made their way to a classroom on the far end of the building and sat at a long table, where Ashley was doling out papers in stacks. "Morning," she said, her eyes flicking to Jack's tooth and then away. "Here are some additional study materials about the Mormons. Read them over and let me know if you have any questions. I'll see what I can find out for you." She motioned toward the insulated coffee mug Molly carried with her. "And you'll need to say goodbye to that."

"What? Why?"

"Mormons don't drink coffee."

"But we're not really becoming Mormons," Molly said patiently. "We're just pretending."

"Coffee drinking is a habit that's too hard to hide," Ashley pointed out. "And the odor—"

"That's *aroma,*" Molly interrupted. "The smell of coffee is not an odor."

"And that is where we disagree," Jack said. Molly ignored him.

"The aroma is difficult to mask. It's best if you give up the habit, Agent North." Ashley didn't leave any room for doubting her seriousness.

"But . . ." Molly was flabbergasted. "But I *need* my coffee."

Ashley shrugged. "I'm sorry."

Molly wrapped her hands protectively around her cup. "What if I only drank it at home, when no one could see me, and kept the coffee maker under the counter when I wasn't using it?"

"Mormons are very friendly—they like to stop by and visit. They'd be able to smell it in your home."

"What are they, bloodhounds?" Molly tried to imagine a world without coffee. It was gray, and bleak, and dismal, and very, very tired all the time.

"You can give it up, Molly," Jack said. "Shouldn't be that hard."

"Says the man who never drinks it. You just don't understand."

"I understand that it's not good for you, and I've been telling you so for years."

"Fine. You're getting your wish." She pushed her coffee away, thinking she might as well get the separation anxiety over with, but then she thought better of it and decided to enjoy every last sip. She grabbed the mug and clutched it to her chest like it was a long-lost child.

"We'd better get to work," Jack said.

Molly looked over the papers for several minutes and then glanced at him. His mouth twitched as he read, and she rolled her eyes. She turned to the next sheet and found she couldn't concentrate. It was all just too complicated. "Are you sure we can't pretend to be non-Mormons? There are such people in Utah, aren't there?"

Ashley lifted one shoulder. Maybe Molly's question didn't call for a full-on shrug this time. "From what I understand, if the Mormons find out you aren't members, they'll spend all their time trying to convert you. They'll bring you casseroles and cookies and just keep showing up on your doorstep every minute of every day. So it's really best if you pretend to be one of them already—otherwise, they could get in the way of your investigation."

"They sound so creepy." Molly suppressed a shudder. She liked cookies as much as the next person, but the thought of someone just knocking on her door any time of the day or night put her nerves on edge. She would definitely have to scout out their new house, make sure all the security features were up to par. They couldn't let someone dangerous get past just because that person was carrying chocolate.

"There is one thing, though," Ashley said. "We've decided it's best if you and Jack pretend to be fairly new members. This way, if anyone questions you about something and you don't know the answer, it won't be obvious that you're bluffing. And you won't have to pretend to have been inside one of their temples."

"I like that. It gives us an out if we forget something," Molly said.

"Well, not only that, but temples are special to the Mormons," Jack put in, "and we'd run the risk of not showing proper respect. I might not believe in their religion, but I don't want to make fun of it."

Molly flashed him a look. All the irritation she'd been feeling toward him vanished, like a snowflake landing on a hot skillet. She wished he wouldn't be so wonderful and lovable when he was getting ready to divorce her. It just made everything so much harder. "How do you know all that?" she asked.

"Don't you remember any of this from training? Molly, the FBI studies all the major religions of the world. You know how many terrorists spring up from fanatical religious factions."

"I sort of vaguely remember that," she said. "It was a long time ago . . ."

"And you were probably daydreaming about guns," he finished for her.

"Yeah, I probably was. Guns are a lot more exciting than all this spiritual stuff."

Jack rose from the table as Ashley gathered their study materials. Molly believed she could now correctly determine the difference between a deacon and a teacher, although she was still not sure about Mia Maids and was unclear on how Beehives worked into all this. She stretched her arms high above her head and stood.

"What's next on our agenda?" she asked.

Ashley consulted a sheet. "Lunch, and then you begin your floral-design training, Agent North. Agent Coleman,

Special Agent Blevins wants to meet you down on the weapons range."

"So Jack gets to play with guns while I'm stuck making flowers? Where is the fairness here?"

"Don't worry, Molly. I'll tell you all about it later." Jack grinned, and just a little bit of her irritation returned.

Lunch sounded wonderful, and as they neared the cafeteria, Molly decided it smelled wonderful too. She would eat her fill and then see if she couldn't figure out a way to skip flower class and hang out on the weapons range instead.

"Hi! I'm Claire Donnelly, Agent Donnelly's wife." Molly was greeted by a tiny bundle of energy when she walked into the room where her floral class would be held. She'd tried to sneak off in the other direction, but Agent Blevins had caught her in the hallway and redirected her. Dang FBI agents—always watching you.

"Oh, hi. Yeah, I know Todd Donnelly. We've worked together a lot."

"Well, he had nothing but the nicest things to say about you. Come on over here to the counter."

Molly reluctantly trailed behind and found herself faced with a display of implements that suddenly made the dentist's office seem not so bad. Knives, clippers, pins, pliers, and a hot-glue gun—all waiting to do some serious damage.

"Agent Blevins says you really aren't looking forward to this," Claire said, handing Molly an apron.

"He's telling you the truth."

Claire laughed. "Well, just relax and feel your way through it. There's nothing to be scared of, I promise."

"You say that because you're actually domestic and stuff. My idea of homemaking is throwing a pot pie in the microwave."

Claire laughed again. "I'm not a very good cook either, but you don't have to be in order to arrange flowers. You just need a sense of color and balance."

"And this is supposed to comfort me?"

"Let me show you what I mean." Claire lifted a skinny bucket of assorted flowers from the floor and set it on the counter. "These are what we call the mass flowers . . ."

"And furthermore, tulips don't stand up." Molly paced the floor of the room assigned to Jack at the FBI's housing facility. Her room was right next door, but she couldn't sleep until she had vented. "They look like such nice, innocent little flowers, but are they? No. As soon as you put them in a vase, they droop over. They turn on you, like Benedict Arnold."

Jack slipped off his shoes and then, ever a neat freak, placed them side by side in the closet. Molly didn't even have to look to know he'd put the left shoe on the left and the right shoe on the right. Little things like that drove her up a tree. Ha ha ha—a shoe tree. Molly thought about sharing her unintentional mental pun with Jack, but decided he probably wouldn't appreciate it.

"So, you had a hard day? Is this what you're saying?"

Molly scowled at him. "That's what I've been saying for the last ten minutes."

Jack nodded slowly. "I see. You know, I should have figured that out sooner. Like, when you repeated yourself four times in the elevator."

"Are you accusing me of something? Because if you are, I think you could just come out and say it."

"I'm not accusing you of anything. I'm just saying that I'm not sure how spending an afternoon playing with flowers could be all that difficult."

"Maybe you should be the florist and I'll be the assassin." Molly flopped onto the bed and covered her eyes with her arm. "I would love to trade places with you."

"Yeah, I know."

She uncovered her eyes. "Seriously, how much fun did you have today? Tell me."

Jack pulled out a pair of sweats and set them on a chair. Then he reached for his shaving kit and pulled out his toothbrush. He was taking an aggravatingly long time to answer, and she knew he was hiding something. Something good.

"It was a lot of fun," he said at last. "They brought in some new guns and I got to try them out."

Molly picked up a pillow and threw it at him. "You got to shoot new guns while I was stuck thorning roses?"

"I imagine you were de-thorning them, weren't you? Removing the thorns, rather than putting them on?"

"Just tell me about the guns."

"They're pretty sweet. They're Glocks, like our old ones, but they're quieter. They'll bring you in to try yours out on Thursday."

"But this is Tuesday. How am I supposed to wait that long?"

"I told them it might be hard for you, but they said they really need you concentrating on your other studies right now."

"Like I *can* concentrate." Molly picked up the blue book next to her on the bed. "Have you tried to read this?"

"I read the first chapter this morning."

"And?" she prodded.

"It appears to be some kind of record of ancient peoples. Uses some of the same language as the Bible, but different, too."

"I couldn't even get past the first little part here." Molly opened the book and turned a few pages. "'I, Nephi, having been born of goodly parents' . . . what kind of name is Nephi? And what are goodly parents, anyway?"

"I imagine he means they're good people." Jack took off his FBI-issued shirt and exchanged it for a clean T-shirt, one that was just a little bit too small and hugged his muscles in all the right places. Molly used to love to see him wear shirts like that, but not anymore. She barely even noticed—really, she hardly even registered—that it was the green one that made his eyes look like a rainforest.

"You look tired," she said, needing to focus on the weariness in his face and not his incredible eyes. It only hurt to think about how handsome he was. He wasn't hers anymore, not really.

"Yeah, I'm pretty beat. After the shooting range, they put me through my paces to make sure I didn't go soft on that last assignment."

"And you passed?" She knew he had. She'd just seen his muscles herself—they were even nicer than before, if at all possible.

"Yeah, I passed." He sat down on the edge of the bed. "Mind if I lie down too? It *is* my bed, you know."

She scooted over a little to make room. He settled back against the pillow, and within seconds, was breathing deeply. That was another thing that drove her nuts. She would lie there half the night, tossing and turning, and he could fall asleep in nothing flat. It just wasn't fair.

She waited a few more minutes, listening to him breathe, and then slipped out and closed the door softly. "Night, Jack," she said through the wall.

FOUR

First on Jack and Molly's schedule the next morning was a meeting with Braden. She wondered what other forms of dental torture he might have devised for them and was vastly relieved to learn he didn't have teeth on his mind at all.

"I'm going to be working with you very closely on this case," he said as Jack and Molly took seats across from him. "I'm not sure you're aware of this, but last year I spent a few months in Utah trying to infiltrate the organization. I . . . was unsuccessful."

"Oh, come on. You're always successful," she said.

"Ordinarily, that's true. But sadly, last year I was not. It was a blow to my ego, that's for sure, but now we have the chance to make it right. By helping you, I get vindication. I can reclaim my man cards."

Molly laughed. "Okay, so what can you share with us?"

Braden filled them in on everything he'd learned the previous year, which wasn't much in regards to the Mafia. He'd made very little headway on that. However, he was filled with praise for certain Mormon traditions—such as cheesy potatoes—and he had nothing but good things to say about the kindness of the people, although his language did turn a bit salty when he mentioned Utah drivers.

"I've been working with the crew out in Utah to help create the command center," he said. "And I know you'll want a lab, Jack. I'm flying out there this afternoon to oversee the final touches on everything. You'll have cameras placed strategically throughout the shop which will patch in to the computers in the basement and also to your laptop so you can keep an eye on things wherever you are. It's going to be awesome. Then I'll come back and help you drive in on Friday."

"That's a lot of back and forth for you," Jack commented.

"It's all right—I like to travel. And you'll need some help with that moving truck and all your stuff."

"We only brought a couple of bags," Molly said.

"But Jason and Sarah Bennett are coming from out of state," Braden pointed out. "You'll need to have more than that with you. The FBI has authorized an expense account—you'll get to go shopping."

"Yippee skippy."

Braden raised an eyebrow. "You aren't going sarcastic now, are you, Molly? I thought all women loved to shop."

"Molly's not all women," Jack inserted.

"I get the feeling I should change the subject," Braden said. "So anyway, we'll fly in to Utah, hit a furniture store and a truck rental place, and continue the trip from there. Makes more sense than driving a truck all the way from California. We'll need to be at the airport by five thirty in the morning."

Molly sighed. "Five thirty . . . without coffee."

"You can do it," Jack said to her, then reached out and shook Braden's hand. "Glad to be working with you again."

"We'll have fun," Braden replied. "Let's go catch ourselves some mobsters."

The next day, after working over at least ten thousand roses—she might have lost count—Molly was finally able to sneak down to the weapons range for some much-needed R & R. A wave of euphoria swept over her, like Christmas and chocolate and a first kiss all at once. She took a deep breath, held it for a moment, and then slowly released it, letting out the stress and anxiety of the last few days. Jack, at her side, chuckled. "Welcome home," he said.

"Thanks."

He might have been joking, but his statement was also very true—this place was like home to her. It was here she felt most like herself. Well, here and anywhere else guns were.

She picked up her new Glock from the table. It was the same style as her old one, but it didn't feel familiar in her hand. She squeezed the grip to get used to the shape and wondered how long it would take to develop a close relationship with this weapon like she had with her old one.

Jack was already putting on his headphones and walking over to the range, but Molly didn't like to rush these things. She hefted the gun a few more times, looking it over, and then reached for the bullets.

"Well, hello there."

The voice had an ingratiating tone, and Molly did a quick character analysis before looking up. Medium height, probably not very attractive, maybe even a little balding on top, too self-confident, and definitely on the prowl. She lifted her chin to see if she was right. Oh, yes—all of the above.

"I see you're racking your gun."

Wow. That was the most inventive pickup line she'd ever heard. She would have to write it down, it was so compelling.

She pasted a smile on her face. "Yes, I am." She wondered for a moment if he was in a leadership position with the Bureau, but meeting his eyes, she knew that was impossible. This was not leadership material here.

"You know, I've found that if I do it this way . . ." He reached over, took her gun, and started to load it. He actually lifted it out of her hands.

Molly was so offended, she couldn't react at first. It was the absolute height of bad manners to take a weapon from someone else's hands—unless you were arresting them or something, of course—and then to imply the person didn't know how to rack it. She literally could not speak for a moment and had to use all her self-control not to put the guy on the ground.

"And that's the easiest way." He handed the gun back with a smile. "My name's Wade Johnson. I just transferred from Langley."

"Ah." That was a safe response, and all Molly could manage.

She grabbed a pair of earplugs and walked over to the range. The new gun was still foreign in her hand and she wanted to get a feel for the backfire before she settled into her practice. She took aim and fired a little high, measuring the kickback and taking note of her needed stance to fire. It was pretty close to her old gun, but would require a little adjustment.

"Let me show you a few things." Wade was at her elbow like a skin disease that would not go away. She handed him the gun wordlessly before he could just take it again.

She watched as he fired a few times, hitting the paper target in the right shoulder twice and totally missing with the third round. He had to be a desk jockey, maybe an analyst. He could not be a field agent.

"It's really pretty simple." He turned back to her. "You try."

Molly raised one eyebrow. This could go one of two ways. She could just put the guy on the ground right now and get it over with, or she could have a little fun and see where this led. She'd been bored the last few days—she could use some entertainment. She stepped to the spot

Wade indicated. He handed her the gun and then came around behind her, standing really close as he showed her how to aim.

So that was his game, was it? She glanced over at Jack, who had a practiced look of concentration on his face. They had agreed when they got married that she needed to handle situations like this on her own—he couldn't go charging in protectively every time someone tried to pick up on her. That might give away their relationship. Of course, if she was in real danger, he'd do whatever he could to keep her safe, just like any good partner.

"Am I doing it right?" Molly asked, deciding to play along—just for the time being.

"Exactly right."

Wade hadn't noticed her incorrect grip. She doubted he was looking at her hands at all. She shifted her fingers and then pulled the trigger.

"Oh, you were a little high. Let me show you." Wade nudged her arm and she made the shot again, this time to the right.

"Here. I'll demonstrate." He took the gun—yes, took the gun—and fired, making a little hole in the target's stomach. There was one bad guy who would need Pepto-Bismol for the rest of his life—way to keep scum off the streets.

"Oh, that's good." Molly batted her eyelashes, then glanced at Jack again. He was supposedly not watching, but a faint smile wrestled with the corners of his mouth. "In fact, that was so good, I think I may just let you have this gun."

"What? Oh, come on now—that's really nice of you, but I can't take it." Wade looked flattered.

"Sure you can. I'll tell the office. I prefer my own anyway." Molly reached back, pulled her gun from under her shirt, took her stance, and pulled the trigger. She drew a perfect smiley face on the target, her first bullet creating one eye, then the other, and the remaining bullet holes forming the smile beneath. She hit the button to slide the target closer so there could be no mistake. Then she holstered the weapon and turned to Wade, who had a look of total incredulity on his face.

"Welcome, Agent Johnson. I hope you'll be very happy here. A few things to clear up for future reference—don't touch my gun, don't touch me, and don't question my ability with a weapon ever again."

She turned, pulled her other gun from the holster on her ankle, and shot a single bullet straight through the heart of the target. Then she strode away.

Jack caught up with her as she marched down the hall. "That was pretty wild."

"Well, he got what he deserved. I can't believe he was ever at Langley—that man is not a professional."

"Maybe you taught him a lesson. I know you've shown me a thing or two in the past."

Molly wasn't sure if that was a compliment or not.

Jack and Molly sat across the table from Tony, studying the young man who was trying to do the right thing and had put himself and his family at terrible risk. Dark circles underscored his eyes, and Molly could tell he was still in pain from his injury. He winced whenever he moved, and he clenched his hand into a fist and pressed it against his back from time to time.

"You said Joe Baker uses a voice changer on his phone. Is there a certain kind or setting?"

Tony shook his head in response to Jack's question. "He must switch it out, though, because he sounds different each time I talk to him."

"So if we weren't able to replicate his voice exactly, it's not that big of a deal."

"That's right. There's no way to replicate it because it's always different."

Jack nodded. "That certainly makes things easier."

Tony slid a piece of paper across the table. "This is the phone number for Fabiano's contact. You need to call as Joe Baker and set up a meeting time. He's expecting you to use the code words 'red' and 'delivery' in the same sentence. Once he hears those words, he'll discuss what he needs from you."

Jack nodded. "And when should I call?"

Tony glanced at his watch, presumably to check the date. "Saturday night at six. There's about a five-minute window, but try to be as close to six as you can. And use a burner phone."

"Of course." Jack patted his pocket. "I've already got it."

"Good."

Jack and Molly stayed with Tony for another two hours, asking him every question that came to mind. By the time they were done, Molly felt sure she could recite not only the inner workings of Scarlotti's organization, but the names of all his pets and his pets' grandchildren as well.

"Thanks for your help, Tony." Jack rose and shook the other man's hand. "You've made the right choice."

"I hope so. For my mama's sake."

"We have mamas too, Tony. We're not going to let anything happen to yours."

As Molly and Jack left Tony's room, she looked back and saw the young man slump onto his bed. "He's really not feeling well," she said. "This has been hard on him."

"But he's alive. He's got to be grateful for that. We've found mobsters' bodies in Dumpsters, in rivers, dead in their own beds—Tony's lucky."

"So are we, to have this chance." They reached Molly's room and she leaned up against the wall before turning the knob. "For some reason, I'm a little uptight about this assignment."

"You? Uptight? I don't believe it."

"I don't either. But it's true."

"You know we're totally up for the challenge. We've been preparing for something like this our entire careers."

"Yeah, I know. And maybe that's why I'm nervous. All that time preparing for a break like this—and then if we blow it, we've wasted our lives."

Jack rested a hand on her shoulder. "Get some sleep. You're worn out. And by tomorrow when we leave, you'll be back in the right frame of mind." He met her gaze. "I need you, Molly."

For a moment she wondered if he was referring to their marriage, but he went on. "You're the best partner an agent could have, but you've gotta get your head in the game, all right?"

She nodded.

"Good. I'll see you in the morning."

Jack stepped into his own room and shut the door, and Molly stayed in the hall for a minute. He only wanted to work with her. Okay—she'd be the best possible partner ever. It was time to snap out of it.

FIVE

"Don't say it. Just don't even say it."

Jack turned to Molly with a benign expression on his face. "Say what?"

"Anything that has to do with the range last night."

"Why would I say anything about it? It's not your fault that Mr. Dude-from-Langley couldn't behave himself around you."

Molly walked a little farther into the furniture store and paused in front of a couch. "And if Mr. I'm-Your-Husband hadn't found it so amusing, maybe I wouldn't be so annoyed right now."

"It was amusing. I was excessively diverted."

"And you don't get to watch my Jane Austen movies anymore if you're just going to use them against me."

Jack came to her side and touched the back of the couch. "So? What about this one?"

Molly studied the fabric's pattern. "It's so . . . floral."

"And you're a florist. The problem?"

Molly sighed. "I'm just not into this, Jack. I mean, yes, we need to pick out some furniture for the house and it should be fun and all, but this isn't my thing. You know that. Can't we just go arrest some bad guys instead?"

"You can't move to a new town without bringing stuff with you. We need some stuff to bring."

"Let's have Braden pick it out. He lived in Omni last year—he knows what floats there."

"You should pick it out so you don't hate everything."

"But this is what I keep saying. I don't care."

Jack sighed. "Do you want me to do it?"

"Would you?" Jack's taste had always been impeccable, so much better than her own. "That would be great."

"Fine." Jack walked through the display, and Molly wandered behind him, mute. They had flown in to Salt Lake International Airport and were now visiting a used furniture store because while Jack and Molly had an expense account, Jason and Sarah Bennett couldn't afford new furniture. Two things struck Molly as funny—first, her new last name was Bennett, and Jack had just been quoting Jane Austen. Second, she had never been in a used furniture store in her life. Whenever she needed something, she just ran into the nearest department store. She realized she might be considered somewhat of a snob, but that wasn't her intention—she just didn't have time to browse and make thoughtful decisions, and, as she had already admitted to herself, she didn't care. Whatever was sitting on the front row of the store was just fine with her.

The text signal on her phone sounded and she checked the display. "Braden rented a U-Haul and he's parked out front," she relayed. "As soon as we're done, we can load up."

"Shouldn't take too long—it's only a one-bedroom house." Jack spoke from a reclining position on a black leather couch in the corner. "And I just found what we want."

"That *is* a pretty set," Molly said, running her hand across the back of the love seat.

"And it's comfortable." Jack closed his eyes again. "I'll be able to sleep on it without a problem."

His tone was completely casual and he didn't say anything more, but Molly caught his meaning. He planned to sleep in the living room in the first home they had ever been able to share as husband and wife, and it broke her heart.

"Now turn to the right. Great."

The photographer couldn't have any idea how awkward Molly felt, standing in his studio wearing a gorgeous wedding dress. And hopefully he didn't know that the dress was rented, or that the bouquet she held was thrown together in ten minutes at the grocery store's floral department.

"Face this way." The photographer rolled a full-length mirror toward her and positioned it so it wouldn't catch glare from the lights. "Pretend you're checking yourself out in the mirror on the morning of your wedding day. This is one of our most popular poses."

Molly turned and caught her reflection. When she'd put on the dress in the changing room, she had only given herself a cursory glance, figuring that whatever the hairstylist had done to her was bound to be loads better than anything she could have done herself.

She hadn't been invested in this part of the process at all. When Braden told her that Mormons like to put wedding pictures on their living room walls and that it would be weird if she didn't have one, she figured she'd just go along with it. But as she saw herself in the dress she'd hastily grabbed off the rack, saw the way the white satin flowed down her body and the veil framed her cheeks, she caught her breath.

The wedding chapel in Mexico where she had married Jack was down a side street from the hotel where their suspect was expected to show up. They only had twenty minutes and they dashed into the church, traded vows and a kiss, and then went on to make the arrest. There had been no fancy dress or beautiful flowers. Molly had always thought they could make up for that later, but as FBI agents married on the sly, they *couldn't* make up for it. That wedding chapel became all she thought she'd ever have, but now . . . She studied herself in the mirror. She looked like a bride. A real bride.

"Perfect expression on your face," the photographer said as he blinded her with a flash.

Molly glanced over to the corner of the room where Jack waited. The photographer had been reluctant to let him in to the session until Jack explained he'd already seen the dress and that no rules of superstition were being broken. She wished she could see Jack's eyes. They always told her what she needed to know. Was he thinking about their rushed wedding too? Did he ever wish they'd had time for a real ceremony, or was he wishing they'd never gotten married in the first place?

When the photographer finally turned off the light that shone in Molly's face, she glanced at Jack. She thought he liked the way she looked, but she wasn't sure, and then his cell phone rang and he was back to business. Just like she should be.

She slipped out of the dress and pulled her own clothing back on, adjusting her weapons in their holsters and feeling remarkably better now that they were in their rightful place. Some women felt naked without jewelry or makeup. She felt naked without her guns. Yeah, she knew it was weird.

Jack guided the car around the bends in the canyon road while Molly watched the screen on the GPS unit. "And there's the turnoff."

"Omni—five miles," she read aloud from the green-and-white sign at the edge of the road. From here on out, it was a straight shot. Soon she would be seeing just what on earth she was getting herself into—flying out to the middle of nowhere, pretending to be some kind of religious zealot, arranging stupid flowers in stupid vases. Claire had been very patient, explaining the same things over and over, but Molly just wasn't getting it. She twisted her simple wedding band around on her finger, not used to the feel of it, wishing she were able to wear such a thing in real life, every day.

She turned around to make sure the U-Haul truck was still behind them. Braden was posing as Molly's brother for his part in the investigation. She had to admit—buying furniture to fill up the van had been pretty fun, once she turned the actual selection process over to Jack. They had come up with everything they wanted except a good entertainment center. She figured she could keep looking once they were settled.

"Main Street, USA," Jack said as they entered the city limits, and Molly gasped. It was so Andy Griffith. She'd never seen anything like it.

Houses were neatly arranged in rows, each with fall flowers lining the porches. Children scampered on the sidewalks, some playing hopscotch, others chasing dogs. A teenage boy raked leaves on an expansive front lawn. An older man waved at their car as they drove by.

"Do we know him?" Molly asked.

"People from small towns are just friendly," Jack said.

She studied the GPS screen again, but there was really no need. Two blocks later, right on Main Street, they saw a sign: "Omni Orchids."

"Honey, we're home." Jack parked the car in front of the establishment, and Molly heard the brakes of the U-Haul squeak as it came to a stop behind them.

"So, this is it." She looked through the window but made no move to get out.

"Yep, here we are." Jack unbuckled his seatbelt. "Are you coming?"

"Um, okay." Molly slowly picked up her purse and took her time climbing out of the car. This was the threshold. Once she crossed it, she was Sarah Bennett, and she couldn't be anyone else until the day they left. She'd done this before and she'd always enjoyed it, but this time, she didn't feel as though she had a grasp on who she was supposed to be.

They pushed open the door of the shop and were greeted by a workman in overalls. He was on the round side, with thinning hair and a kind smile. "You must be the Bennetts," he said, stepping forward to shake hands. "I'm Roger Ferguson. I've been overseeing the painting and redecorating of the place."

"Good to meet you, Roger," Jack said. "Yes, we're the Bennetts. I'm Jason, and this is Sarah."

Molly found her hand enveloped in Roger's huge paw. "Welcome to Omni." He pumped her arm up and down. "We're just a small community, but we're growing every year. I'm sure you know we have a Walmart."

Molly nodded and tried to look impressed.

"And just last month, we got ourselves an Arby's. It's down Main here about four blocks. You can't miss it—huge cowboy-hat sign, about yay big."

"We like Arby's," Jack said. "Maybe that's what we'll do for dinner tonight. What do you think, Sarah?"

"I'd love it. I don't want to cook until I've unpacked the whole kitchen," Molly replied. She inwardly grimaced.

She'd rather not unpack the kitchen at all, ever. Could she get away with that?

"Well, I'll let you two look around. Have you been over to your house yet? I understand you've bought the old Tyler home."

"We came straight here. Sarah couldn't wait to see the shop."

"Let me know if you want me to change anything. I'm just doing some touching up on the paint."

"So, um, Roger . . ." Molly decided to take the plunge and start getting to know the locals. "Are you a Mormon?"

Roger puffed out his chest. "Yes, ma'am. In fact, Brigham Young is my great-great-great . . ." He paused and started counting on his fingers. "Well, I forget how many 'great's it is, but he's my uncle. We talked about it in FHE before my son went into the MTC. I checked it out against New FamilySearch when I was putting something on TempleReady from the SSDI, and now it's on my FamilyTreeMaker. I told my HP group leader about it at my PPI, and he was blown away."

"I bet he was," Molly said for lack of a better response. "I'll take a look around now, thanks."

As they turned the corner to the back of the building, Jack whispered, "What was that all about?"

"I don't know. I think he was saying something about his cholesterol levels." She stifled a yawn. She really wanted some coffee. No, scratch that—she'd fight Jackie Chan with her bare hands for some coffee. And the Tylenol she'd taken hadn't even touched her withdrawal headache.

The shop was larger than Molly had envisioned, with a long work counter, a good-sized walk-in cooler, and storage in the back. Off to the side was a little room with tables and chairs. Here, customers would discuss what they needed for weddings and funerals, Molly presumed by looking at the books laid out on display. They were filled with pictures of gorgeous arrangements, and she felt a stab of dread. She would never be able to replicate any of those beautiful pieces.

"So, how does it look?" Roger asked as they reentered the lobby area.

"I think you did a lovely job," Molly said. "It looks great."

"Well, we're glad you bought the place. When Esther retired, we were all a bit discouraged. This little shop brought a piece of class to the town, and we hated to lose it. But now you're here, and we couldn't be more tickled." He motioned with his arm. "This place was built to withstand all Mother Nature's fury. The brick walls are covered by a thick layer of mortar. The floors are concrete, the ceiling joists are thick wooden beams—if we ever have a tornado, you'll be as snug as a bug."

"That's good to know," Jack said.

Roger fished in his pocket and came out with a business card, which he handed to Jack. "If you find a spot I missed, why, you give me a call."

"Thank you, Roger. We appreciate it."

Braden entered the shop just as Roger was exiting, and he held the door open while the older man maneuvered his toolbox and paint through. Once he was gone, Braden said, "I just checked in with Agent Blevins. He said to let you know he's sending in someone to help out—kind of an insider who can show you the ropes."

"That would be great," Molly said. "I hope it's Claire. I didn't get nearly enough practice with calla lilies." She'd been too busy trying to figure out roses, and they never made it to several other varieties of flowers. Claire said Molly was making it too complicated—she was probably right.

Braden rubbed his hands together. "Now let me show you the place. It's amazing."

"It is?" Molly glanced around. The plum-and-sage wallpaper—still purple and green to her—had turned out nicely, and she really liked the white trim, but she wouldn't necessarily say it was amazing.

Braden threw the deadbolt on the front door, rattled it to make sure it was locked, and said, "Follow me."

He steered them past the walk-in cooler and into the storage area, then reached behind a shelving unit and pushed something. A section of wall slid back, revealing a staircase that led down sharply. "After you," he said, gesturing toward Molly.

She ducked through the entrance and headed down, grateful a light had automatically come on. She hated going into dark places unprotected, but she knew the guys would laugh at her if she pulled the gun she wore at the small of her back. Once she reached the bottom of the stairs, she turned around in wonder.

"You said there would be a command center, but this is a lot nicer than I was expecting," she said as Braden and Jack joined her. "This really is amazing."

"Pretty awesome, huh? Our carpenters did all this down here, and then we hired Roger to do the upstairs. Bring some business to the locals, that sort of thing."

"So he doesn't know about any of this?" Molly asked.

"Nope."

A bank of computers covering one wall showed camera images of the shop from different angles, the street outside, and a house she presumed to be their new abode. She walked over to study the shot of the front lawn. Sure enough, marigolds edged their walkway too. What did this town need with a florist? It was practically crawling with flowers, even though the weather would soon turn cold.

Braden grinned. "And check this out." He pulled open a wall panel to reveal a supply of ammo and a few extra guns. "You're all set to go."

"Looks like it." Jack picked up one of the guns, looked it over expertly, and then replaced it. "The FBI thought of everything."

"Well, I hate to toot my own horn and all that, but I did have some input," Braden said.

They climbed the stairs and slid the panel back into place. Molly stuck her head in the cooler as they passed, noting that it was completely empty. She took a long breath. "So, when do we open for business?"

"Wednesday," Braden replied. "Tonight, spend some time getting settled in your new house. Tomorrow, place your floral order and touch base with Fabiano's contact. Then go be a Mormon on Sunday. Monday morning, you'll set up the shop, and by Wednesday, you'll be ready to open."

"What? So soon?" Fear clutched at Molly's chest. "But that's . . . so soon."

"Yeah, you said that." Braden sounded amused. "We don't have the luxury of taking our time—we're already running behind schedule. Fabiano's men are expecting to see a fully functioning shop when they come in. You've got to give every appearance of being on task."

"I know. I just thought . . ." She paused, trying to get the whine out of her voice. She was thirty years old, for goodness' sake. She could be mature about this. "I just thought I'd have more time to practice." She would absolutely not be the weak link in this operation. If her substandard floral skills did anything to blow their cover, she'd never forgive herself. A florist who can't floral? Yeah, that was really going to convince the people of Omni that she and Jack were who they said they were.

"Time for practice is over," Jack said. "Now let's get to the house and unload the truck."

They drove the two blocks to their new home, and Braden pulled the U-Haul into the driveway. Jack unlocked the front door with the key Agent Blevins had given them. Molly walked inside and liked the place instantly. It felt comfortable, like good people had lived there in the past. The hallways weren't too pinched, the rooms were spacious, and there was a ton of closet space. Maybe she could've brought all her clothes—she didn't have to put the leopard ones in front.

"Molly, did you see this kitchen?" Jack entered the bedroom and found her contemplating the built-in shoe rack.

"Kitchen?"

"Yeah, you know—the room with the fridge in it?"

"Ha ha." She was no Martha Stewart—or Paula Deen, for that matter—but she could identify a kitchen in a lineup. "No, I haven't been to that side of the house."

"Well, it's awesome. Stainless-steel appliances, the works."

"I'll take a look in a bit." She'd make it over there eventually, but it just didn't seem like a priority.

They walked back outside to the truck, where Braden had rolled out the ramp and was getting ready to put the dolly to good use. Just then, they heard a voice.

"Well, I'll be. I heard the house got sold, but I said I wouldn't believe it until I saw it. And here you are, right in front of my eyes."

Molly turned and saw a middle-aged man standing on the sidewalk, studying them with a big smile on his face. "Hello," she said cautiously. "We're the Bennetts."

"And I'm Clive Godfrey. Welcome to Omni." He stepped forward and shook their hands, a bit more vigorously than Molly really liked. "Indeed, welcome." He then stepped back and pulled out a cell phone, pressed a few numbers, and held it to his ear. "They're here," he said and then hung up. It seemed a very suspicious call.

Molly's apprehension was justified when just two minutes later, ten cars converged upon their street. Men poured out of the vehicles like bees from a hive—hey, maybe that's why she and Jack had studied beehives before coming here—and swarmed all over the truck, grabbing boxes and carting them away.

Molly edged toward Jack. "Sweetie, what's going on?" She lowered her voice. "Are we being robbed?"

"I don't think so." He craned his neck to look. "I think they're helping us move in."

"Oh." She really had no other response. She just stood there and watched as the men darted back and forth, grabbing everything they could get their hands on and whisking it away. The entire truck was unloaded in less than ten minutes—not that it had been completely full, but still. She felt like she needed to sit down and catch her breath.

Another car pulled up, this one driven by a woman. She opened the back door of her vehicle and lifted out a large picnic basket.

"Hello!" she called out cheerfully. "I'm Elsie Young. Welcome to the neighborhood!"

"Thank you." Molly nearly dropped the basket when it was offered—she hadn't expected it to be so heavy.

"Now, you're Sarah Bennett, and your husband is Jason—is that right? Are there any little Bennetts running around somewhere?"

"We weren't able to have children." Molly smiled around the words. That was one thing about herself that was the truth, no matter how deep her disguise. Her mind flashed back to a white-walled hospital room, the smell of antiseptic, the scramble of nurses and doctors to pull the bullet from her lower abdomen and stop the bleeding. Jack watching anxiously, begging her not to die. There would be no children.

"Oh. Oh, I'm sorry. Well, it's a one-bedroom house anyway. That's why it took so long to sell—most people wanted more rooms." Elsie reached out and squeezed Molly's shoulder. Molly disliked being touched by strangers and found it hard not to duck away. She smiled, hoping she looked gracious, and wondered if the touching thing was typical of Mormons in general or just this one.

"Well, there's enough food in the basket to make a couple of days' worth of meals, and you let me know if you need anything else. I can have a whole turkey dinner over here at a moment's notice."

"You can?"

"Okay, maybe I'd need a couple of hours' notice. Don't want to eat undercooked turkey, do we?" Elsie laughed. "That wouldn't be a good welcome to Omni."

"No, it definitely wouldn't."

"I'll go now and let you get settled, but please do call. My number is on a card inside the basket. There's a magnet on the back so you can hang it on the fridge." Elsie bustled around her car and opened the door. "We'll see you at church! Our ward starts at nine."

She drove away, leaving Molly holding a very heavy picnic basket and wondering for the hundredth time that day what on earth she was doing in Utah.

"Now that I have given you the sum total of my knowledge concerning this place, it's time for me to head back to HQ," Braden said. "Agent Blevins has me working with Tony to hunt down additional evidence on

Scarlotti. But I've got your security cameras patched in to my computer so I can help watch for any suspicious mob activity, and I'll come back whenever you need me."

"Thanks for all your help." Jack bumped knuckles with the other agent.

"No problem. And I'll call with details about my investigation into Scarlotti—now that we've got Tony on our side, this should go much faster." Braden paused at the door. "So, uh, guess you want me to return this U-Haul, huh?" He ducked when Molly threw a newly unpacked throw pillow at him.

SIX

Molly arched her back to straighten the kinks. She had been working since early that morning, taking inventory of the shop and finding out what she needed to order. There was a note on the whiteboard telling her where to find a paycheck for an employee who'd been on vacation, and she'd found plenty of ribbon, wire, and floral tape, plus some gadgets she couldn't identify. It looked like her first supply order would be mostly flowers.

Claire had made her a list of suggested varieties, and Molly supposed she could just start at the top and order a few of everything. She picked up the phone and was about to start dialing the floral wholesaler when she heard a tap on the front door. She thought about ignoring it, but it wasn't one of those timid "I'll go away if you don't answer" taps.

A woman with shoulder-length brown hair peered through the glass of the front door and waved when she saw Molly coming closer. She held up a Styrofoam cup, and Molly caught her breath. She needed one of those.

She glanced up and down the street as she flipped the lock. She didn't see any suspicious mob-types hanging around, so she opened the door and smiled.

"Hi! I'm Melissa Coon. I run the Hard Book Café next door, and I brought you a little 'welcome to the neighborhood' present." She handed the cup to Molly, who couldn't bring it to her lips fast enough.

It took her a second to register the taste—it wasn't at all what she had expected. "It's not coffee."

A shadow crossed Melissa's face. "Um, yeah. It's hot chocolate. I mean, I *can* make coffee, and I do—but I don't get many orders for it. I just assumed . . ."

Molly could have kicked herself. She'd been so excited to see the cup, she lost focus. "Oh, that's not what I meant," she said quickly. "I'm so *glad* it's not coffee. I didn't want to turn down your generous gift, but I really do prefer hot chocolate, and this is honestly some of the best I've ever had." Now that she knew what it was and her taste buds weren't prepared for something else, she could tell that yes, this really was very good hot chocolate. "Thank you."

Melissa's expression went back to normal. "You're welcome! So, what was your name?"

"I'm Sarah Bennett, and my husband's Jason. He's unpacking at the house right now." For a second, Molly wondered if she should feel guilty about that. Wasn't it the wife's job to put the house together? But he was so much better at it than she was. Why deny him the satisfaction?

"Well, I hope you can stop in sometime soon. If I don't have the book you want, I can order it, and we have free Wi-Fi and everything."

"That sounds great. And thanks again for the hot chocolate."

"No problem!"

After Melissa said goodbye, Molly locked the door and went back to work. The hot chocolate actually was giving her a little bit of a buzz—she didn't know it was the sugar or the theobromine, but it was helping stave off her coffee craving. She called the wholesaler, placed her order, and then decided there was nothing more she could do here. It was time to go home and spend the rest of Saturday pretending to be domestic.

Just as she tucked her purse under her arm, she heard another tap and sighed. What was it with this place? Did a Closed sign not mean anything anymore?

A tall, pimply-faced teenage boy stood on the other side of the door. Molly opened it just a crack and said, "Hi. Can I help you?"

"Um, yeah. My name's Ryan and I used to work here. Esther said she left my last paycheck in the register."

"Oh, that's right." Molly opened the door the rest of the way and let him in. Then she turned on the register and withdrew the check. "Here you go."

"Thanks." Ryan shifted from one foot to the other and then cleared his throat. "I worked for Esther for two years, doing deliveries and putting away shipments and stuff. If you need any help, I'm kind of out of a job now, what with her selling the shop and all . . ."

Molly looked him over. He seemed like a decent kid—a little on the gangly side, maybe, but she couldn't hold that against him. "I'll talk to my husband about it," she said. "Can you come back Monday morning? The floral delivery will be here around ten, so if you came then and we decided to hire you, you could get right to work."

Ryan grinned, exposing a smile that looked as though it had recently benefited from the miracles of orthodontia. "That'd be great."

Once he left, Molly locked the door again, hoping she would actually make it out of the building. This time, she was successful.

"I don't have any objection." Jack closed his laptop. "I can't find anything in this kid's background that would keep us from hiring him."

"Okay, let's give him a try. Of course, we don't know if we'll get enough business to justify having an employee." Molly flung herself backward on the couch and covered her eyes with her arm. "What if no one comes in? What if we just sit there, day after day, with no customers?"

"Molly, it doesn't matter how many customers we get. We're here to take down Scarlotti's organization, remember? The flowers aren't important."

She sighed. She hadn't forgotten—she just didn't want the shop to lose credibility. They'd hardly look like a real business if no one came in. "Anyway, I placed the order, so we're good to go." She sat up and looked around. "You got a lot done today."

"Yeah, we didn't bring much with us, so it didn't take me very long."

She liked how Jack had arranged the pictures and put the new black vase on the end table. He'd made the place look homey.

"Oh, and I warmed up some of the leftover food from last night," he said.

Molly followed him into the kitchen. "Wow! It looks great in here, too."

"See? The kitchen is not an evil place."

"Yes, it is. You just made it look less evil, that's all." She sat at the table and accepted the plate Jack handed her. "Are you chewing okay with that tooth?"

He nodded. "Yeah, it's fine."

They ate in silence for several minutes, Molly relishing every bite of this homemade dinner that came from someone else's home. "Do you . . . do you think we really need to go to church tomorrow?"

Jack sighed. "I don't know. I mean, we've been working hard all day—it would make sense if we stayed home and rested, and then went next week. On the other hand, I don't want to blow our cover."

Molly loved the idea of staying home. The bed was soft and comfy, the blankets were warm and cuddly . . . She yawned. Going to bed early and sleeping all day sounded like heaven.

"We'd better go," Jack said at last. "The case is the most important thing."

"Elsie said church starts at nine. That's nine in the morning."

"Nine at night would be an awkward time to begin church services, don't you think?"

"Oh, hush up." She finished eating and then rinsed her dishes and stacked them in the dishwasher. "It's almost six. Better get ready to make that phone call."

Jack clipped the voice changer over the mouthpiece of the burner phone, and they waited in silence as the clock ticked down the remaining minutes. Molly tapped her nails on the countertop. The sooner they established contact, the sooner they could make their arrests, and the sooner she could get out of this tiny town and away from these infernal flowers. Omni didn't even have a decent shooting range. It was probably best that she hadn't Googled that before she came—she might have turned down the case.

"This is Joe Baker," Jack said into the phone a moment later. "I'm calling to discuss the delivery of your red tulips."

He listened for another moment. "Yes, that's correct. You'll find me at Omni Orchids on Main Street." Another pause. "Fine." Then he hung up.

"Well?" In her impatience, Molly felt a little like bouncing up and down.

"He's coming in sometime next week. He'll place an order for eighteen red tulips in a crystal vase—that's how we'll know it's him. Then he'll set up a time for us to meet Fabiano in person."

"Tulips! Why does it always have to be tulips?" Molly groaned.

"I'm sorry, but they were the first red thing I could think of that we'd deliver. The code words, remember?"

"This is why people have partners. You can confer with your partner and get better ideas." Molly slumped down on the bar stool at the counter. "I don't know if we even have any crystal vases at the shop. I know we have some large ones, but I didn't check to see what they're made of."

"You can order one, I'm sure."

"Yeah, I guess." Molly rested her chin on her hands. "You could have suggested a nice poinsettia. They're red."

"And it's not winter," Jack reminded her.

"It's close enough. Or roses."

"I thought you hated taking off the thorns."

"Okay, okay, I give. Tulips. Stupid, droopy tulips. Whatever. But don't think I'm just going to forget this." She paused. "I'm going to bed."

"Okay."

She hesitated in the doorway. "If you want the bed tonight, I can take the couch."

"No, go ahead. I'm comfortable out here."

She opened her mouth, wanting to say more, but then walked into the bedroom and closed the door behind her.

SEVEN

Molly turned off her hair dryer at the sound of someone knocking. Jack was taking a shower, so she grabbed her gun and edged toward the door. A glance at the monitor showing the front porch revealed an elderly woman in a purple dress. Molly couldn't holster her gun—she was still in her bathrobe—so she tucked it in the silk plant in the foyer, close at hand but hidden, and opened the door.

"Good morning," the woman greeted her.

"Um, hi," Molly said. "Can I help you with something?"

The woman chuckled. "You can't do anything for me today, my dear. I'm here to discuss what I can do for you."

"I'm already a Mormon," Molly blurted, "so I don't need a new set of scriptures or anything. In fact, I'm getting ready for church right now."

The woman chuckled again. "It's all right. You see, I got a phone call on Friday from a very nice man named

Special Agent Blevins. He sent me down here to help you out—said you needed Mormon lessons."

Molly raised an eyebrow. *This* was the person Braden told them was coming? This tiny little woman with the bright eyes and the pink shoes was their expert?

"I know I'm not what you expected," the visitor said. "But I promise I'm telling the truth. Why don't you call your headquarters and get the skinny? I can entertain myself while you make the call. Oh, and by the way, let me introduce myself." She held out a blue-veined hand. "My name is Ida Mae Babbitt Gilmore."

Ida Mae sat across the kitchen table from Jack and Molly, eating one of Elsie's amazing caramel brownies. "I hate to admit it, but these are even better than mine." She scooped the crumbs off the table and dusted them back onto her plate. "And I don't say things like that every day."

Molly had called Agent Blevins, and he confirmed Ida Mae's story with a bit of humor in his voice. Molly didn't know what to think. How could this elderly woman be a spy in her own right? She couldn't picture Ida Mae toting a gun or tearing after a criminal during a high-speed chase, yet Blevins said this woman and her friends had solved five cases with very little help from local law enforcement.

"So, Mrs. Gilmore—" Jack began, but she held up her hand.

"First of all, you're a Mormon now, so the correct term is 'Sister Gilmore.' But that's not good enough either. You have my permission to call me Ida Mae."

He nodded. "All right. Ida Mae, what do you propose to do for us?"

"Well, we need to get you absorbed into Omni's Mormon society. I'm sure Elsie told you we meet for church at nine."

"That's right," Molly said.

"I dislike the nine o'clock schedule, personally. It throws off my meal plans for the whole day. If I want a roast for dinner, I have to put it in right after I walk in the door. If I put it in before I go to church, then it's done for lunch, and I don't care for roast at lunchtime. It's a dinner food. Oh, but I've probably confused you. I'm sorry. We only get the little roasts because there's just the two of us. So they cook faster than they would if we were making a large one."

"Oh." The size of the roast didn't mean a thing to Molly.

"My wife isn't much of a cook." Jack cast a quick look her direction. "We tend to go with a frozen dinner on Sunday."

"But not like a TV dinner," Molly hastened to add. "More like a lasagna or something."

"Well, I'll have you over one night soon," Ida Mae promised. "I would invite you today, but George and I are going to a special meeting in Salt Lake City right after church and won't be back until late. Sundays are just crazy for us."

"Why is that?" Molly asked.

"Oh, didn't I tell you? George is the bishop of our ward."

Jack sent Molly another look, this one filled with concern. "He is?"

"Yes, he is, but it's all right. You don't need to worry about fooling him. I already told him about you, and he's more than willing to help."

"The . . . the bishop is going to help us pretend to be Mormons?" Molly blinked. This little old woman was full of surprises.

"Oh, yes. He thinks it's going to be great fun. But we have to be careful with what assignments you're given and so forth. We can pretend, but only to a certain point, you understand."

"We understand, Ida Mae. We don't want to poke fun at your beliefs."

Ida Mae turned to Jack. "I appreciate that, young man. Now, we've only got half an hour before church starts, so let me fill you in on some basic things you'll need to know."

"How early should we get there?" Jack asked. "I'm nearly ready, and I think it will only take Sarah another few minutes—"

Ida Mae held up her hand. "That, my dear boy, is the first lesson of Mormonism. Never show up early. Unless you're a deacon, or the family of a deacon, or perhaps the organist. The rank and file show up right on time, or five minutes late."

"Late?" Molly saw Jack flinch as he repeated the word. Punctuality was coded into his DNA.

"I know it's not ideal, but try as we might, for some reason we just can't pull together an entire congregation on time. We've come to accept it as one of those funny little quirks of ours."

"So you admit that you're quirky?" Molly asked.

Ida Mae laughed. "Oh, gracious, yes. That's what makes us so wonderful. Now, let's see. You'd probably better sit in the back, on the right. All the benches toward the front are taken. Not officially, mind you—we don't have assigned seating, but everyone tends to gravitate to the same spots week after week. And ignore the flying Cheerios. The Peterson twins are going through a stage, but they'll outgrow it."

"Should we be taking notes?" Molly asked.

"No need. It will all be burned into your brain after one week."

Ida Mae went on to explain that the day would be broken up into three segments. "I recommend not raising your hand in Sunday School. Brother Ewell is a wonderful man, but he enjoys delivering lectures rather than teaching classes, and interruptions tend to annoy him. Just flip around in your scriptures a lot and look studious. That's the best way to manage that class. Now, as for priesthood and Relief Society . . ." She paused. "Jason, it's too bad my nephew isn't in the ward anymore. He could walk you through it quite well. As it is, we'll just wing it, shall we? They'll ask you questions about your business, and where you moved from, and I'm sure you've got that down pat. But if sports comes up, you'd probably better like basketball. You do like basketball, don't you?"

Jack shrugged. "I don't have time to watch sports, really."

"Well, I guess saving the world does cut down on one's free time. To be safe, say you're a fan of BYU, but you wish Jimmer was still on the team."

"BYU, Jimmer—got it," Jack said.

Ida Mae turned to Molly. "And what are your hobbies, dear?"

"Uh, they aren't what you might consider . . . traditional."

Ida Mae laughed. "Agent Blevins already told me you're one of his top weapons experts. I didn't imagine you'd spend your time clipping coupons or knitting."

"Agent Blevins said that? That's really nice of him. I do spend a lot of time on the range."

"Anything else?"

"Um, I like to go shopping."

"For clothes," Jack inserted.

"Well, of course for clothes," Molly said. "What else would I mean?"

"Groceries, maybe?"

"Oh, yeah. No, I don't grocery shop. Or furniture shop. Or . . ." Molly thought for a minute. "Yeah, clothes are about it."

Ida Mae leaned forward a little. "There's one more thing. Agent Blevins told me the two of you are married in real life. He worried that I'd be scandalized at the thought of two agents living together without being legal."

"Well, we spent quite a lot of time together before we were married and got along just fine," Jack said.

"Ah, but you did get married later, and that's quite romantic. Anyway, I just thought I'd tell you that I'm in on your little secret. I think it's positively wonderful. You know, I met my husband George on a case."

"You did?" Molly was astounded.

"I did. In fact, he tackled the bad guy and made it possible for us to catch him." Ida Mae's eyes had gone dreamy, but she blinked and came back to the present. "George ended up having another knee surgery, but all's well that ends well, right?"

"Um, sure." Molly glanced at the clock. "Oh, we'd better get going. Ida Mae, would you mind coming with me to see what I've chosen to wear? I want to get it right on our very first Sunday as Mormons."

"Certainly, my dear." Ida Mae rose from the table and followed her down the hall.

As they entered the bedroom, Molly glanced over at the bed and realized she hadn't made it yet. That was actually nothing new—bed making wasn't on her list of priorities—but now she saw it through Ida Mae's eyes and hoped the woman wouldn't think she was a total slob. Okay, maybe she *was* a total slob—but for some reason, Ida Mae's opinion mattered to her, and she felt as though she'd come down a notch on the respectability scale.

Molly pulled out her navy skirt and white blouse, and then held up her navy flats. "What do you think?" She'd gone for the most reserved outfit she owned and hoped it was good enough. If not, she could wear her trench coat over the ensemble, but it was still quite warm out, and she was sure to melt before the day ended.

"Um . . ." A crease wrinkled Ida Mae's already wrinkled forehead. "That's nice, dear. But I wonder . . . do you mind?" She motioned toward the closet.

"No, not at all." Molly stepped to the side and let Ida Mae peruse her wardrobe. She wondered if she should have packed more turtlenecks.

Ida Mae turned around. "I don't mean to criticize your fashion taste, my dear, and I hope you don't take this the wrong way, but your outfit is just a little—shall we say, boring." She held up Molly's bright red high heels and a red-and-blue paisley shawl. "Let's throw these into the mix, shall we?"

"Sure, we can do that." Molly took the items and chuckled. "I was just trying to be conservative."

"Well, there's conservative, and then there's Barbara Bush," Ida Mae replied. "Don't get me wrong—Barbara's a lovely woman, but we don't need to look like her all the time, do we?"

"No, I guess not. Thank you. I'll get changed right now."

"I'll leave you to it, then. And remember, be five minutes late."

"Ida Mae? Tell me about the sacrament. From what I read, you should only take it if you're a member—but won't it look funny if we don't take it?"

Ida Mae paused in the doorway. "Are you a good actress, Sarah? I'm sure you must be—you are an undercover agent and all. I just wondered if you would be up to faking a coughing fit in the middle of the sacrament service today."

"A coughing fit? That would be pretty disruptive, wouldn't it?"

"Exactly." Ida Mae smiled. "And then you'd have to slip out, and Jason would have to follow you to make sure you're okay, and by the time you recovered, you would have missed the sacrament entirely."

Molly nodded. "And that way, I don't have to pretend to take it, or refuse it."

"Exactly," Ida Mae said again. She stepped forward and placed her hand on Molly's arm. "I think it's wonderful that you and Jason are being so careful not to make fun of our religion. When Agent Blevins called and told me you were coming, I really didn't expect you to be so considerate."

Molly's face grew a bit warm. "Really, it's nothing—"

"It's something to me." Ida Mae gave her another pat and moved back to the doorway. "We'll come up with another distraction next week."

Molly waited until the bedroom door closed and then dressed quickly, smiling as she put on the red heels she had thought might be a little too daring for this quiet town.

EIGHT

George Gilmore was possibly the cutest little old man Molly had ever seen. He was completely bald on top, had just a faint fringe of white decorating the sides and back of his head, and his eyes twinkled like Christmas lights. Molly tried to reconcile the man seated on the stand in the chapel, smiling at the congregation as they filed in—five minutes late—with the man who had tackled a dangerous assailant. She had to wonder if Ida Mae had just been exaggerating when she told them the story of her husband's escapades. There was so much about the situation that was hard to believe.

Molly glanced around the chapel at the Mormons. As she greeted them in the foyer, Ida Mae had whispered something that sounded like "Just relax. It doesn't get really weird until they bring out the chicken." Did she mean a live chicken, like an animal sacrifice done Ozzy Ozbourne style, or did she mean fried chicken, like a friendly picnic in the middle of the meeting? Molly had no idea and she fidgeted a little in her seat, wondering what to expect.

Three young men up at the front of the room began to do something with bread, and Molly realized this was her cue. She coughed a little, and then a little more, trying to sound dainty and covering her mouth. She didn't want to disrupt this part of the meeting, which was obviously pretty important, but she didn't have any bright ideas of her own and decided to run with Ida Mae's suggestion. She coughed a little louder, then stood and slipped out of the bench, Jack close behind.

She walked down the hall to the drinking fountain and took a few big swallows, then turned to catch a glimpse of a young man with a tray in the foyer.

"Are . . . are they following us?" she whispered to Jack. "Are they going to hunt us down and make us take it?"

"I think they're just offering it to the people sitting near the doors," Jack replied. "I don't think they're coming down the hall."

"Oh. Okay."

They waited in the hall, Molly emitting an occasional cough for appearance's sake, until after the water was passed and George's voice came over the speaker in the ceiling, thanking the boys for passing the sacrament. Jack and Molly walked back into the chapel, Molly feeling distinctly awkward at having disrupted the meeting twice—once while leaving, and once coming back in. She wondered if the Mormons were going to judge her for it, but as she sat, a warm, frail hand landed on her shoulder.

"Here you go, sweetie." She was passed a cough drop, and turned to face the elderly woman who offered it. "I always keep some in my purse," the woman whispered.

"Thank you," Molly whispered back, then unwrapped the drop and popped it into her mouth. It tasted a little odd, sort of like pennies and lint and like it had been in that purse for a long time. But she couldn't deny the kindness of the gesture.

The meeting came to an end with no chickens, and Molly was disappointed. She'd been hoping for something really spectacular, but . . . nothing. They'd sung a few songs, told some woman she had to work in the nursery now, and then a couple of people stood up to give talks. No chicken. Not even a feather. About the time the closing hymn was announced, Molly realized what Ida Mae had done—she'd helped make the meeting seem perfectly ordinary to take the edge off Molly's nerves. Sneaky trick, that.

Sunday School was all right. The teacher talked a lot about the Bible, which Molly had read once. She was able to nod intelligently from time to time, which seemed to be all the teacher wanted. But then it was time for the men and women to go to their separate classes.

"Why do you think that is?" Molly whispered to Jack. "Are they going to tell you stuff they don't want us to know?"

"I doubt it. They probably just want to give the lessons in a girly way for you and a manly way for me."

"Oh, come on." She playfully slugged his shoulder. "Seriously, why?"

He shrugged. "Go find out."

She walked down the hall where all the women seemed to be heading and caught sight of Ida Mae, chatting with two other ladies. She waved when she saw Molly, and bustled over when the crowd thinned enough to allow for bustling.

"Sarah, I'd like you to meet my two friends. This is Arlette Morgan, and this is Tansy Smith." Ida Mae leaned in a little. "They're the other members of the Secret Sisters," she said conspiratorially.

Molly blinked. This was just getting weirder and weirder. She decided the best way to cope was to go along with it.

"Hi." She wiggled her fingers in her own version of a wave.

"Hi," Arlette and Tansy chorused.

Arlette was a rather dour-looking woman who wore a cardigan sweater over her dress. She had wrinkles around her lips, the kind that come from years of silently expressing disapproval. Tansy was actually bouncing a little bit on the balls of her feet. She had a happy grin on her face and reached out to grasp Molly's arm.

"We know why you're in town," she said, giving a not-very-subtle wink. "And we're so excited to help you."

Molly cast her eyes in Ida Mae's direction. "They know?"

"Well, of course, dear. I wouldn't dream of embarking on an adventure without them."

Molly glanced around to see who might be listening, but the crowd seemed to have disappeared, probably into the rooms that lined the hall. "Maybe I need to explain what it means to be undercover. The more people who know why we're here, the greater the chance that we won't be able to do our jobs."

Ida Mae patted her arm. "Don't worry, Sarah. It goes no further than the three of us. And George." She paused. "Hmm. I suppose I have told rather a lot of people. But trust me—you'll be glad of it before this is over."

Molly had doubts. Serious doubts.

"Sundays are exhausting." Molly took off her shoes and lay down on the couch. "I've never seen anything like it. Was that a church or a circus?"

"Church," Jack replied. "There weren't any elephants." He sat on the ottoman near her feet and began to rub them, just like he had in the old days. She wasn't about to stop him, a feeling of nostalgia rising in her chest and making her long for what they'd lost.

A knock sounded at the door, and Jack rose to answer it. Molly inwardly groaned. Her left foot felt wonderful, but he hadn't made it to her right foot yet, and it felt neglected.

"Hi! I'm Brother Jacobsen, and we wondered if you'd like to come over to our house for dinner tonight. Nothing fancy—just fried chicken and rolls and a veggie tray and apple pie, maybe a little pasta salad and some homemade ice cream. Whaddya say?"

Molly stood and glanced over Jack's shoulder at the short, pudgy man on their porch. He certainly looked friendly enough.

"We just live right down the street there, in the house with green trim. We usually eat around five. My wife is quite the cook, and we'd love to welcome you into the neighborhood. Whaddya say?"

Jack took a deep breath and plunged in before their visitor could take up his campaign again. "That sounds delicious. Can we bring anything?"

"Oh, no—my wife always makes enough to feed the armies of Helaman. Plus, you're just settling in—I bet your kitchen's not even unpacked yet. We'll take care of everything. See you at five!" He took a step back, but lost his footing and stumbled a little.

"Are you all right?" Jack asked.

"Oh, sure. Weebles wobble, but they don't fall down, as the saying goes!" He laughed heartily as he made his way down the sidewalk.

"Looks like we've got a dinner date," Jack said as he closed the door. "But I've got to have a nap first."

"I can't argue with that," Molly said. "But I feel like I need to take a coma, not just a nap."

She wandered into the bedroom and changed into some sweats, then flopped onto the bed, face down, and started to drool on her pillow. Being a Mormon really took a lot out of a person.

NINE

Molly woke up the next morning with a food hangover. She'd never eaten so much in one meal in her entire life. Sister Jacobsen was one amazing cook and kept passing the serving dishes to Molly, and the next thing Molly knew, she was utterly, totally, and completely full to the gills. She practically had to be pushed home in a wheelbarrow, and now, waking up to the results the next morning, she was a little bloated and a lot happy. Maybe there was something to this cooking thing after all if it could release those kinds of endorphins in the brain. But then she realized she'd actually have to step foot in a kitchen, and changed her mind.

As she sat up, the craving for coffee hit her like a football tackle. She'd always consumed most of her coffee in the mornings, and there was just something emotionally encoded in her that associated sunrise with java. She could probably drive to a nearby town, hit a Starbucks, then change her clothes and brush her teeth and no one would know, but that sure seemed like a lot of hassle just to hide a cup of coffee. She could keep powering through this, right? And if she was crankier than the Wicked Witch of—take your pick, East or West—while she was at it, well, she'd just blame that on the Mormons.

She wandered out to the kitchen and said good morning to Jack. He was rubbing his neck as though he'd gotten a kink in it. If the stubborn man would just sleep in the bed like a normal person . . .

Jack got in the shower. Molly knew he'd be in there for a long time—whenever he got an ache, he liked to stand in the hot water spray and soak out the soreness. She had a few minutes alone, and suddenly, she didn't *want* to power through this coffee withdrawal. She wanted to surrender, name it the victor, and be done with it.

She grabbed her purse and then tiptoed back into the kitchen. She hoped that turning on the faucet wouldn't change the water pressure in the shower—all she needed was for Jack's nice hot water to turn cold. Must keep Jack happy. Closing her eyes and hoping for the best, she turned on the faucet and filled up a mug. She didn't hear any yelps, so she figured she was still safe.

While the microwave warmed her water, she crept to the door of the bathroom to make sure the shower was still going, then went back to the kitchen to take the contraband out of her purse. A single-serving packet of coffee was hiding under her wallet, and she pulled it out with a crazy grin on her face. "My precious," Molly hissed as she tore off the top, then sniffed the amazing aroma as it wafted upwards.

She stopped the microwave before the timer went off and took out the steaming mug, then poured in the crystals and stirred. She smiled as the water turned a rich, dark brown.

The first sip made her taste buds break out into song. She wished she had time to savor every last molecule, but Jack would be getting out of the shower soon, so she drank down the rest, swished the cup out with hot water and soap before putting it in the dishwasher, tucked the empty packet back in her purse so she could dispose of it in a public restroom or Dumpster later, and stuck a piece of gum in her mouth. Then she lit a match and waved it in the air. By the time Jack got out of the shower, she was curled up on the couch with a book.

"Nice try, Molly, but it's not going to work."

"Hmm?" She looked up from the page she hadn't even bothered to read. "I'm sorry—what did you say?"

"The match? Come on—how junior high is that? Now, where is it?"

"What? I don't know what you're talking about."

He put one hand on his hip. "Pass it over."

She knew that look, and she knew there was no fooling him. With a sigh, she got up, grabbed her purse from the bedroom, and handed him the packet.

"Is this all you had?"

"Yes."

"You don't have any more tucked away somewhere?"

"No."

"If I search your room, what will I find?"

"You'd have to get a warrant."

"I can get a warrant."

"I know." Molly slumped back on the couch. "It was just one cup, Jack. One little tiny itty-bitty cup."

"And I can smell it. And that means anyone else can smell it too."

"Fine. Just . . . fine."

"I know this is hard on you, Molly," Jack said, his voice suddenly soft, "but you know this is important, right? This case—we're not going to get another chance. This could make our careers or send us right back into obscurity."

"Yeah, I know." She sighed, playing with the tassel on one of the throw pillows. "It's just . . . coffee is so good."

"It's actually pretty nasty."

"No! It's wonderful! And it's warm, and soothing, and it makes me happy . . ."

"And you'll go through some withdrawals, but then you'll be fine."

"Fine? Can there be such a thing as fine in a world without coffee?"

"The Mormons do all right without it."

"Yes, but they have God. So this proves that the only thing more awesome than coffee is God."

Jack chuckled. "Hang in there."

Molly burrowed deeper into the couch. She didn't want to hang in there. She wanted coffee.

The floral delivery truck arrived right at ten, followed closely by Ryan. Molly told him he was hired and put him to work filling buckets with water to put the flowers away.

"I'm sure Esther and I were trained in two completely different ways," she told him, "so our methods are likely to be different." She mentally crossed her fingers, hoping he'd accept her explanation and not notice how very clumsy and inexperienced she was.

"Not a problem. I just do as I'm told." Ryan carried a stack of buckets over to the deep sink in the corner, and Molly began taking the flowers out of their boxes.

The walk-in cooler had two sets of shelves on casters, and she thought it would be easier to arrange the flowers the way she wanted if she pulled a shelving unit out into the main room, placed the buckets on it, and wheeled it back in. She had fun putting all the red flowers to the left and then working through the rainbow, finishing up with blue on the right, then went to push the shelving unit back in while Ryan carried the empty boxes out to the Dumpster.

"Um, a little help here?"

Jack walked over from where he'd been dusting shelves in the front of the shop. "Yeah?"

"Can you help me push this back in?" Molly asked. "It's pretty heavy, with all these buckets on it."

He tilted his head to the side. "And you loaded it up out here why?"

"Don't tease me. Just help me. I was trying to be organized, okay?"

He shrugged and took hold of one end of the shelving unit, and together they pushed it toward the cooler. Molly propped the door open with a garbage can, and they were nearly there when she lost her grip and the unit slid into the wall, knocking out a chunk of plaster.

"Oh, crud!" Ryan came in the back door and gaped at the hole. "What're you doing?"

"I guess I'm redecorating," Molly said. "The distressed look is in."

"I don't think that means actual holes, does it?" Ryan was the one who looked distressed. "I mean, Esther would have a cow."

"We'll fix it." Jack pulled his wallet from his pocket. "I've got Roger's card right here."

Molly and Ryan pushed the rack the rest of the way into the cooler while Jack made the call. "I promise, I'll keep the shelves where they go from now on," Molly told Ryan. "I just wasn't expecting them to be so heavy." He threw her a look of incredulity, and she had to agree. She really hadn't thought it through much at all.

"Roger can't make it, but his brother, John, will be here first thing in the morning," Jack said. "Roger still has the key from when they were doing the painting, so John will just let himself in around seven."

"I guess that's all right." It bothered Molly that Roger hadn't returned the key, but they hadn't brought any money in yet to stock the till, and as long as she got the key back the next morning, she could let it go. She'd just make sure the security cameras were on before she left the building.

That night, Molly dreamed she was being chased around the floral shop by a bouquet of roses with extra-long thorns. The accompanying card was decidedly uncomplimentary. She woke with a start and automatically reached over for Jack, but he wasn't there. She could hear him snoring softly on the couch, too far away.

TEN

Molly had meant to be ready for the shop at seven. There was just something about the handyman being there by himself that didn't sit right with her. But she couldn't find one of her shoes, and she couldn't wear the outfit she had on with the shoes she could find, so she had to change her clothes. Jack wasn't amused. She tried to remember—had he always looked so grumpy when it took her this long to get dressed, or was that new? At any rate, it was seven thirty when they reached the shop, and considering she was without her coffee, Molly thought that only being thirty minutes late was a miracle. Jack unlocked the back door.

"Hello?" He pushed the door open and stepped inside. "Huh. There's no one here."

Molly stepped across the threshold and immediately sniffed. Something hung in the air, a lingering residue. "A gun's been fired in here."

She and Jack drew their weapons and began to edge their way through the building without turning on the interior lights. The fine hairs on her arms prickled as she moved in and out of the shadowy corners. John should have been there, fixing the wall, but the shop looked deserted.

"All clear," Jack said from the other side of the sales display area, then stepped toward the back of the building, working in a circle.

Molly crossed to the front of the store. "There's a repair truck out front, but I don't see anyone sitting in it. Maybe he finished up here, then went next door for some hot chocolate." She walked over to the wall and noticed that a large trash can had been pushed in front of the hole. She tugged it away, then gasped. "What on earth?"

The hole in the wall was not only still there, but it was twice as big. It looked as if a whole brick that had been behind the mortar was now gone.

She bent down to peer into the gap. She knew she wasn't the most coordinated person in the world, and sure, she had smacked the wall pretty hard with that shelving unit, but the nick she'd made was absolutely nothing compared to this. Why had John decided to knock out such a huge piece of plaster just to fix what was essentially a scratch? Give her a bucket of spackle and some paint, and she could have fixed it herself.

"It was hardly even visible," she muttered.

She straightened, her senses on full alert. A gun had been fired. John dug a hole in the wall and was now nowhere to be found, even though his truck was out front. What was going on?

"Molly." The tone in Jack's voice told her he'd found something. She came to his side, peering over his shoulder into the cooler. A pair of legs stuck out from beneath a shelf.

"Scoot over." She stepped into the cooler, flexing her fingers around the grip of her gun. As she drew closer, she saw that the man who lay on the floor was dead, a bullet hole in his back.

"What have you got?" Jack asked.

"It looks like a .44 short-range shot—I'd say no more than ten feet. Clean into his heart from the back. That's just a guess, though—we need the ME to call it for sure."

"I don't need the ME to call it. You're always right." Jack pulled out his cell and pushed a button. "Special Agent Blevins, please." He waited, shifting from foot to foot impatiently. "This is Jack," he said at last. "We've had an incident."

He outlined the situation while Molly continued to inspect the body visually. The man wore old clothes—ratty jeans, a T-shirt with more holes than a pool table, and paint-splattered work boots. He was obviously John, the missing painter. But who would want to shoot a painter, and in a floral shop?

Jack hung up. "He's sending the local uniforms. We need to treat this as though we're Jason and Sarah Bennett, unfortunate souls who just found a dead body in their cooler. The FBI will stay apprised of the case, but we can't blow our cover by bringing in all our own guys."

Molly nodded and stepped out of the cooler, then flipped on the shop lights. "He was shot right here," she said, pointing to the wall with the hole. That's where she had smelled the gunpowder when they first walked in. "Someone came up behind him while he was working. Why?" She stepped over to the area and saw what she had missed in the shadows—blood splatter on the wall. No doubt about it. And the floor rug was gone.

"A shot through the back and into the heart is Scarlotti's signature hit," Jack pointed out. "Was he trying to send us a message of some kind?"

"Why does Scarlotti keep a hit man on retainer when he enjoys doing it himself?" Molly pulled out a stool and sat on it, her brain whirling furiously.

"Maybe this has nothing to do with Scarlotti. What do we really know about John?"

"Nothing, except that he's Roger's brother, and we know nothing about Roger." Molly stood and crossed the room to look at the hole again. "Why was this entire brick removed? If I were going to patch a wall, I'd fill it in, not take stuff out."

"Was the brick damaged?" Jack asked. "Maybe the shelving unit cracked the brick, and he had to replace it."

"But where's the brick?" Molly looked around. "It's not on the floor." She glanced into the garbage can. "And he didn't throw it away. If he had just taken it out, it would still be here."

"Unless someone wanted that brick."

Molly raised an eyebrow. "Why would someone want a brick badly enough to kill for it? That doesn't seem right—it's just a brick."

"Hang on a second." Jack fumbled in his pocket and pulled out his keys. A flashlight, tiny and deceptively powerful, dangled off the chain. He crouched down and shone the light into the hole. "Get me a baggie, would you?"

Molly glanced around the shop and spied a box of small plastic bags. She grabbed one and brought it over. Jack used it to wipe the inside of the hole, then turned the bag inside out. When he held it up to the light, Molly could see traces of fine white powder clinging to the sides.

"Dust from the mortar?"

"Possibly, but I don't think so," Jack said. "I'm going to take this downstairs and see what we've got."

"Bet you a pizza it's cocaine."

"I'd take you up on that, but you'll probably win."

Molly nodded. "What about the local cops?"

"I left just enough powder in there for them to find. They should be all right."

Jack opened the door to the command center and slipped through it. Not ten seconds later, sirens sounded outside and two police cars pulled up, flanking an ambulance. Jack returned and closed the basement door snugly. "I'll get to it later," he said.

He and Molly gave their statements to the police, then stood out of the way as the crime-scene photographer took all the necessary pictures before the body could be moved. As they waited, Molly heard a knock on the shop's front door. A glance showed Melissa peering in through the glass, a bag in one hand and a cup in the other.

"What's going on?" she asked as Molly opened the door. "Why are the police here?"

"We've had . . . well, we've had an incident." Molly used the same word Jack had earlier, not sure what else to call it. "Um, someone was killed."

"Oh, no!" Melissa set down the cup on an end table near the door, but clutched the bag a little tighter. "What happened? Who was it?"

"I'm really not sure. The police will tell us when they know. Jason found him in the cooler when we got here."

"It was John, wasn't it? He called this morning and ordered two of my special cinnamon rolls and a hot chocolate." Melissa held the bag up higher. "I was just bringing them over when I saw the police."

"He called you? What time?"

"About forty-five minutes ago. I would have been here sooner, but the store got really busy and I couldn't leave until Janie came in to run the till."

"I think the police will want to talk to you," Molly said, resisting the urge to question Melissa herself. "Maybe John said something that would be helpful."

"I don't think he did—we just talked about his order. But sure, yeah, I'll talk to them."

As if on cue, one of the uniformed officers walked toward them. "Mrs. Bennett, the victim's driver's license identifies him as John Ferguson. Your husband said John had been brought in to repair a wall."

"That's right. And this is Melissa Coon, from next door—she spoke with John this morning."

The officer turned to Melissa. "Can I ask you some questions, ma'am?"

Molly stepped away to give Melissa some privacy with the officer. She had no doubt she could get the same information from Melissa later, and didn't want to seem too nosy. She joined Jack where he leaned against the counter.

"They swept out the hole in the wall," he said softly.

"Good." She could see the tension in his shoulders. "You're dying to get down there and run your own tests, aren't you?"

"Yeah. I wish they'd hurry and leave."

The officer who had been speaking to Melissa thanked her and walked away. She still clutched her bag as if it held the answers to all the questions of the universe.

"I just can't believe he's dead. I mean, I made these for him." She held the sack a little higher. "Oh, and Sarah, to find him in your cooler! Are you all right?"

Dead bodies were a part of Molly's job, but she had to confess, she was rattled—and Sarah Bennett ought to be a total wreck. "I'll be okay. You just don't expect . . . this sort of thing. You know?"

Melissa wrapped an arm around Molly's shoulders. "Bless your heart. Here, take these. They're still warm." She thrust the sack into Molly's hands. "And this is the same kind of hot chocolate I brought you before. You look like you could use a pick-me-up." She gave Molly a little squeeze, then reached out to grab the door handle. "I've got to get back, but please, if you need anything, just call me, okay?"

"Okay. Thanks, Melissa." Molly felt a little awkward, standing there holding a dead man's breakfast, but after a moment, curiosity overcame her and she opened the bag. Oh, wow. These weren't just cinnamon rolls—they were works of art. She stepped into the wedding consultation area, out of sight of the police, and dug in.

"You know, you don't have to hide," Jack said from behind her. "People eat when they're stressed all the time."

"But I'm enjoying this a little too much," she replied, handing the second roll to him.

Jack chewed and swallowed his first bite. "I see what you mean. Got any milk?"

"Hot chocolate." She passed him the cup.

Five minutes later, buzzing from a chocolate/sugar high and feeling much better, Molly rejoined the police in the main area of the shop, Jack right behind her. The officers were swabbing up some of the splattered blood, and Molly remembered what she was going to tell them.

"I don't know if it matters, but the rug that goes here is missing, and it would probably have blood on it too," she said.

The officer in charge, a kindly man named Bates, told one of the other men to begin a search for the rug. Moments later, it was found in the Dumpster. "Get it bagged. Oh, and Mrs. Bennett, I wouldn't go outside for a minute. The rug is . . . a bit soiled. You don't need to see it."

"Okay, I'll stay in here," Molly promised.

About a half hour later, the medical examiner arrived and entered the cooler. Jack and Molly tried to stay out of the way, but they were also straining to hear what was being said.

"Mr. and Mrs. Bennett, we'll be in touch with any further questions," Officer Bates said after the ME had finished his examination. "We appreciate your cooperation in this matter. We assure you, things like this don't happen very often in Omni. In fact, until last year, we didn't have a full police force, but operated with a county sheriff and a few deputies."

"The town is growing, then," Jack commented.

"Yessir. I'm sure you know we have a Walmart."

"We did hear that, and we plan to get over there as soon as we can."

"We also just got an Arby's."

Molly could do nothing but nod.

The body, now in a black plastic bag, was taken out to the medical examiner's vehicle, and after the police finished up with a few more questions and one last sweep of the area, everyone was gone.

"You can go play now, Jack," Molly said, and he was through the door and down the stairs in a matter of seconds.

She paused to collect her thoughts. So far, the day certainly hadn't gone how she'd intended, and she needed to pull her mental to-do list back in front of her. First, she thought she'd call Ryan.

He picked up on the second ring. "Yeah?"

"Hi, Ryan. This is Sarah Bennett. We've had a little bit of chaos around here this morning, and I need some time to get organized. Can you come in tomorrow morning instead of today? I don't think I'll have much for you until then."

"Do you need any help?"

"No, it's stuff I've got to do myself. But we'll see you tomorrow, okay? Bright and early—it's our grand opening, of course."

"Okay." He sounded a little disappointed, and she couldn't blame him. She'd overheard him tell Jack about a used car he was saving up to buy. She wished she could pay him for the time he'd miss because of the murder, but that wasn't something a typical business owner could afford to do. And she couldn't have him underfoot while they investigated.

She grabbed a bucket, a mop, and a bottle of bleach and got to work on the cooler floor. She didn't want any trace left behind. She gave it two extra-good scrubbings, then did the same in the work area where the shooting had actually taken place. After that, she took the bucket and mop out to the Dumpster. No way would she be using those again.

ELEVEN

After making sure the doors were locked, Molly headed down to the command center to see how Jack was getting along with that sample. He was on the phone when she joined him.

"Yeah, it's definitely cocaine. Let me know." He snapped his phone shut. "That was Special Agent Blevins. He's in touch with the local uniforms, and he'll be our go-between while we figure this out."

"You owe me a pizza." Molly plopped down on the couch in the corner. "But why would cocaine be in the wall of the floral shop?"

"I never took you up on the bet. And Scarlotti must have been using the shop to relay the stuff to his customers," Jack said. "He found out somehow that someone was in here messing with the wall, and he came in here to make sure John couldn't call the police."

"I don't buy that it was Scarlotti. Not without more evidence. All we have to go on is the way John was shot, and that could just be a coincidence."

"Okay, I'll give you that, but we need to keep it on the drawing board."

"I won't discount him entirely, but I'm not ready to finger him." Molly thought for a minute. "And who stores loose cocaine in a wall? If I were putting drugs in a hiding place, I'd make sure they were securely wrapped up. It just doesn't make sense to me that there was residue in the hole. I think it was put there to make us assume the murder was drug-related."

"So John was killed for some other reason, then?"

"Could be."

"It's possible." Jack sat down at the computer and started tapping keys. "I checked the security cameras, and the tapes from this morning are fuzzy. I don't know why. Braden pulled the feed up on his computer back at HQ. I'm going to work on them from this side too, and we'll teleconference with our findings."

"And I have a floral shop to open for business tomorrow." Molly stood and stretched. "Nothing like a cadaver in the cooler to throw one off one's groove."

Jack didn't reply, but she didn't expect him to. He was already deep in thought, poring over the computer screen.

Molly spent the next few minutes wandering around the shop, looking for anything else she might want to mop up or scrub down. It was a delay tactic, and she knew it. She didn't want to move on to the next task, but she had to face the inevitable and get to work. She touched the gun at the small of her back, trying to feel grounded, then pulled out a vase and filled it with water. She set it on the counter in front of her, then stared at it. Claire had taught her that the flowers would speak to her as she became more accustomed to them, and Molly wondered just when that might be.

"Okay," she said aloud. "Greenery first."

She stepped into the cooler, careful not to slip where the floor was still damp from the mopping, and grabbed a bundle each of leather leaf and tree fern from the box in the corner. She put several sprigs of each into the vase, wondering why they kept spinning around and wouldn't face the direction she placed them. Maybe after she got the flowers in, they'd hold still. Some beautiful peach roses had come in with the shipment—she'd start with those.

The stems were too long, of course, so she trimmed them down, only to find that she'd cut them too short. What had Claire said about holding the flower up in front of the vase to measure before cutting? Molly couldn't remember how that was all supposed to work. Something about using her eyeballs. Sounded painful.

"Hey, I'm going to run down to Arby's," Jack said, his voice startling her. "Are you hungry?"

"Oh, yeah. Get me a combo, would you?"

"Be right back."

After twenty agonizing minutes, all twelve roses were in the vase, and Molly was in tears. No matter what she did, the arrangement looked terrible. She wasn't cut out for this.

She had tried to tell Agent Blevins, but he seemed to think it was the easiest thing in the world, and she wished he'd sent Claire and her husband instead. It didn't matter that Todd was a red-haired Irishman and therefore looked nothing like Joe Baker—they could have made it work, right?

Molly grabbed one of the bows Esther had left behind and jammed it into the vase. It was like putting a silk negligee on a Jersey cow—didn't matter how you dressed it up, it was still ugly. She pulled her gun out of its holster, took a stance, and leveled the barrel at the vase.

"So, you're gonna be a wise guy, are you? You're gonna mess with my head, are you? Well, go ahead. Make my day."

She heard the back door to the shop open behind her. "Sarah?" Jack came to her side, and she caught the scent of roast beef from the sack he held. "Honey, we can't shoot the flowers."

"Why not? They're exhibiting suspicious behavior."

"I'm sure they are, but I don't think shooting them is the answer. Besides, we have a visitor."

Molly realized he'd called her "Sarah," and he'd only do that if someone else was with him. Feeling sheepish, she turned and found herself meeting the bright eyes of Ida Mae Gilmore.

"I wasn't really going to shoot the flowers." She returned the gun to its holster. "I was mighty tempted, but I wouldn't have gone through with it."

"I imagine it would have been a waste of a good bullet," Ida Mae replied, her voice filled with humor. "Now, let's see what you've got here." She entered the work area, her mouth going slack when she saw the vase. "Um, well, the flowers are a very pretty color."

"You don't have to mince words with me. I know I really stink at this." Molly sank onto the stool in the corner. "I don't know what I'm supposed to do. We open tomorrow, and I can't sell stuff like that." She flapped her hand at the offending arrangement.

Ida Mae tapped her lips for a moment. "Esther did most of the arrangements herself when this was her shop, but she did have holiday helpers. You could call them and see if they'd like to work for you."

"I could, couldn't I?" Maybe there was a light at the end of Molly's tunnel.

"Although, I know one of them is due to have a baby next week, and the other is on vacation until the first of the month."

The light became a train, blowing an ear-piercing whistle.

"Let me make a quick call, if I might."

Molly nodded her assent, and Ida Mae dialed. She spoke for a moment, then turned to Molly with a smile on her face. "The cavalry will be here in ten minutes," she announced. "Why don't you eat your lunch, and I'll clean up a little while we wait?" The floor was covered with rose stems and broken pieces of fern, casualties of the war Molly had just waged.

"Oh, I don't know," she said. "I'd feel guilty sitting here eating while you cleaned up my mess."

"Well, what if I told you I already had Arby's for lunch? In fact, I was just leaving when Jason walked in.

We got to talking, and that's why I'm here—I followed him over. And what if I told you that I live to sweep?"

"The broom's over there," Molly said.

The sandwich was heavenly, and Molly felt a lot better now that she'd eaten something a little more substantial than cinnamon rolls and hot chocolate. Not that she meant to be disparaging in any way—cinnamon rolls would always be near the top of her favorite-things-ever list—but she'd needed a serious infusion of protein.

She heard a tap on the back door of the shop, and Ida Mae stepped over to answer it. Tansy and Arlette walked in, and Molly stifled a sigh. If this was Ida Mae's idea of the cavalry, the shop was doomed.

"Oh, my." Tansy pressed a hand to her mouth as she looked at the vase. "Well, I've seen worse. No, that's a lie. This is the worst. But we can fix it."

Ida Mae beamed. "Tansy's a magician with flowers. In fact, she even thought she might buy this place when Esther retired, but she couldn't afford it."

"Do you really think there's hope, Tansy?" Molly asked.

"There's always hope. If there weren't, what would be the point of life?" Tansy pulled the flowers and ferns out of the vase and laid them on the counter. "Oops, there's the first problem."

"What?"

"You didn't use any tape across the top of the vase. Didn't your teacher show you that trick?"

"She might have, but to be honest, it's all a blur." Molly's lesson in vase arrangements had taken place at the same time as Jack's training session with his new gun, and she'd been jealous. Consequently, her mind might not have been entirely on flowers during that hour.

"And because the stems are a little short, we'll use a smaller vase." Tansy grabbed one from the shelf and filled it with water. Then she picked up a roll of waterproof tape and used six-inch strips to make a grid across the top.

"Oh, that does look familiar now," Molly said. "And then you put the stems in the holes of the grid."

"That's right, or you can use loose white foam in the bottom to hold things still, but that tends to clog the rose stems."

Molly surveyed the older woman. "You should have bought the shop, Tansy. You're a natural. I'm just bumbling my way along here."

Tansy reached out and patted her shoulder. "It's all right, dear. We have different talents. I'm sure I'd be no good as an FBI agent."

Molly was still unsettled by the fact that so many people knew she and Jack were working undercover. Maybe they should have just named the shop "FBI Ferns" or "Agents' Asters" and done away with the whole "secret" thing altogether. She wanted to get Agent Blevins' take on it, so after watching Tansy work her magic on the roses, Molly excused herself and stepped outside to make the call.

As soon as Blevins picked up, she said, "Sir, we've got little blue-haired gumshoes running all over the floral shop now, and I'm feeling very uncomfortable about it."

"Ida Mae Gilmore and her friends are completely trustworthy," Agent Blevins told her. "I checked them out carefully before I called Mrs. Gilmore, and I was impressed with their record."

"I don't question your judgment, sir, but I do worry about our covers being compromised."

"I appreciate your concern, Molly, but I think it's unwarranted in this situation. Take what help these ladies can offer you, and later, if you feel that one of them constitutes a security risk, we'll deal with it then. From what I've seen of their work in the past, I think they'd be great FBI agents, and would hire them myself if it weren't for their advanced years."

"They are something else, that's for sure," Molly said. "Tansy went from fixing my floral arrangement to asking about my gun to wanting a signed photograph of James B. Comey, all within about sixty seconds."

Agent Blevins laughed. "You have to admire that kind of dedication. Not many people even know who heads up the FBI, let alone want to hang his picture on their wall."

"It is pretty admirable," Molly admitted. "All right, sir, if you don't feel a little weird about this, I'll proceed."

"It's unorthodox, certainly, but we do need to think outside the box from time to time."

Molly said her goodbyes and hung up, then stepped back into the shop.

"There you are," Tansy said, clasping her hands. "So, are you ready for your next lesson?"

Claire, bless her heart, had tried everything she could to keep Molly's attention focused, but it hadn't worked. Molly admitted that the fault lay solely with herself—she wasn't interested, at all, in flowers, and didn't care if she knew the difference between a stamen and a pistil. Tansy, on the other hand, made this whole flower thing a lot of fun. And Molly found herself enjoying the process, which shocked her.

She was halfway through a second vase arrangement when Ryan came bursting in, his hair sticking up at all angles.

"I know you said not to come in today, but I had to," he said breathlessly, as though he'd been running. "I just heard. Is it true? I mean, it has to be true, but it can't be true, right?"

"Do you want to interpret, Tansy?" Ida Mae asked. "I think he's speaking your language."

"About John Ferguson getting shot in your cooler, I mean," Ryan clarified.

Molly pressed her lips together. She hadn't planned for that bit of information to come out just yet. "Who told you?"

"So it is true." Ryan leaned on the counter and buried his face in his hands. "This is awful. This is just awful."

"John Ferguson was shot in your cooler?" Tansy's eyes were wide.

"He wasn't actually shot in the cooler," Molly said. "He was shot out here, and then dragged into the cooler." She hastened to add, "At least that's what the police think."

"I noticed the rug was missing," Ida Mae said. "Esther had such a nice rug in here."

Molly glanced at Ryan and lowered her voice. "It's been taken in as evidence."

Ida Mae nodded knowingly.

Ryan raised his head. "This just isn't how you run a floral shop," he said miserably. "There shouldn't be dead people in it."

"I know." Molly reached out and patted his elbow. "Were you and John close?"

"I never met him. But still, Sarah, did he have to die in the shop?"

The kid seemed a little hung up on what was and was not proper floral-shop etiquette. Molly had to admit that dead bodies were not on the list of supplies she had thought to order, but Ryan didn't seem to be focusing on the fact that someone—a real, live person—had died. Shouldn't he be more broken up about that?

Ryan wiped his sleeve down his face. "Okay, I'll come back in the morning. I just had to find out. Is . . . is everything . . . ready for tomorrow?"

Molly guessed he was asking about the removal of the body and details like that. "Everything's fine."

"Okay. See ya."

After watching the boy slump out through the door, she turned to Ida Mae. "I'm sorry I didn't mention the . . . incident before."

"That's quite all right, dear. You probably couldn't say anything until the police made a formal announcement."

This lady surprised Molly at every turn. "Yes. I did want to wait, but I guess the wheels of gossip never stop turning."

Arlette chuckled from her seat in the corner, where she'd been knitting a green sock for most of their visit. "We don't have *wheels* of gossip, Sarah. We have spaceships of gossip. They're much faster and more efficient."

Molly finished her arrangement. After getting a nod of approval from Tansy, she set the vase in the display cooler and wiped off her hands.

"Are you feeling ready, dear?" Ida Mae asked.

"As ready as I'll ever get, I suppose," Molly replied. The shop had been dusted until it shone—this was one advantage of being married to someone with OCD—and the cooler was full of flowers. In the back was a bucket of red tulips, just waiting for Fabiano's man to come in and make contact. The sooner, the better, in Molly's opinion.

TWELVE

Molly had enjoyed spending the afternoon with Ida Mae, Tansy, and Arlette. She got a kick out of their banter, their references to cases they'd solved in the past, and their occasional use of terms like "villain" and "sleuthing" that sounded so funny coming from their wrinkled little lips. A few times, Molly had ducked her head or stepped into the cooler to hide a smile. She especially enjoyed the eight floral arrangements Tansy made up and put in the display cooler so there would be a selection for the next day's grand opening. But Molly was more than ready to leave the shop and get back to the case.

She dropped onto the couch and kicked off her shoes. "What a day."

"How'd you get along with your tutors?" Jack asked.

"It was interesting. Tansy does have a way of explaining things, and I think I'm starting to get it, but those ladies . . ." Molly shrugged. "I'm exhausted from listening to them talk. Where do they get their energy?"

"You're probably just having caffeine withdrawals. You'll feel better once it's all out of your system."

"I guess you're right." She decided not to think about caffeine. That might lead to thoughts of coffee, which would lead to thoughts about how much she wanted some, and that was not a safe path to travel. "I have to admit, it's pretty humiliating that we had to bring in some little old ladies to clean up my mess. I'm not cut out for this mission, Jack. I'm only here because I'm your partner."

"And I'm only here because I look like Joe Baker."

"What?" Molly sat up and faced him.

"Think about it. I've been trying to get on this task force for five years, and they've passed me over every time. Now, all of a sudden, they discover that I bear a slight resemblance to the guy they need to impersonate, and they can't wait to send me out into the field. It's not because I'm a good agent or I'm smart or I'm capable. No, it's because I look right." He rearranged the magazines on the coffee table, not because they were messy, but because he was agitated. He loved to clean when he was agitated. "I didn't earn this assignment, Molly. And that really bugs me."

She didn't respond for a minute. She'd been so busy feeling sorry for herself that she hadn't stopped to consider how Jack felt. It was true—this task force was his dream job and he was finally on it, but totally by chance. That would be hard, to get what you want but not to feel you had earned it.

Then she realized something else. It had been a long time since she'd thought about Jack's feelings, much longer than just that day or just this assignment. Her inability to have children had caused her so much internal pain that she'd walled herself off and hadn't reached out to him like she should—not just about having a family, but about everything. She wondered how much that had to do with their current marriage problems.

She stood and crossed the room, then took a seat on the arm of his chair. "I'm sorry," she said, placing a hand on his shoulder. "I didn't realize you felt that way."

He didn't reject her touch. "I'll get over it."

"You know what I think?"

"What?"

"I think you and I should do whatever it takes to prove to Agent Blevins that we're more than capable of doing this assignment. You deserve to be here, regardless of what you look like. And I deserve to be here . . well, let's see." She racked her brain for a minute.

"You deserve to be here because you're a good agent," Jack said.

"You think so?" The heat Molly felt pulsing through his shoulder and into her hand intensified. She was sure she was imagining it, though.

"Yes, I do. And I agree. Let's get this case wrapped up fast so we can impress Agent Blevins, go home, and get on with our lives." He stood up. "What do you want for dinner?"

Molly's hand grew cold as Jack stepped away. She closed her fingers into a fist, trying to preserve the feeling of warmth, but it was gone. "Do we have anything good?"

"I think our picnic basket is empty, and I didn't make it to the store this afternoon. Finding a body in the cooler will do that to a person's schedule."

"Let's just go back to Arby's, then," she said. "We can bring the food here and eat while we keep working."

"Sounds like a plan." Jack grabbed his wallet off the counter, and they headed out the door. Molly hoped a big dollop of Horsey Sauce would help clear out her sinuses. For some strange reason, she suddenly had a case of the sniffles.

"What is the good of having a security system when it can be hacked so easily?" Jack grabbed his hair at the roots. "I thought I was just uploading the data wrong, but Braden can't access it either."

Of course they'd both known something was up with the tapes earlier at the shop, but Molly didn't want to ask Jack about them in front of Ida Mae and the other ladies. Just because they knew about the case didn't mean they needed access to the inner sanctum. But from the tension she'd sensed in Jack, she'd known it wasn't good.

"Everything's either in shadow or blurry." He grabbed his drink and took a long swig through the straw. "It's like the static from one of those old TV sets—you know, the kind that had to warm up? The picture stays half formed and never clarifies."

Molly stepped over to his side so she could see what he meant. The images on his laptop screen were fuzzy and impossible to make out.

"But the system was tested before we even got here, wasn't it?" she asked. "This is crazy."

"And I can't find any evidence of tampering." Jack raked his hand through his hair again, stress radiating off him. "None of our systems were breached, the software's fine—I just can't figure it out."

"Maybe Braden should fly out and take a look."

Jack narrowed his eyes at her.

"I'm sure you're doing a great job—don't get me wrong," she said quickly. "But this kind of thing is his specialty."

"Everything's his specialty. And nothing is mine."

Molly blinked. Jack wasn't usually so pessimistic. That was one of the things that had first drawn her to him—he was level-headed in the worst crisis and could think his way out of anything. He didn't let stuff get him down. He must really be struggling with this to be reacting so negatively.

"You could be right." His voice interrupted her thoughts.

"I am? About what?"

"We should probably have Braden come take a look."

Jack set up a split screen and pulled up Agent Blevins and Braden on their secure webcam channel—sort of like Skype, only a whole lot better. "I can't figure it out on this end, and I think we need some help. Braden, can you come out?"

"I just got home. I haven't even unpacked yet." He sounded cheerful, despite his whiny words.

"You never unpack. You live out of your suitcase," Jack retorted.

"Fine, I'll come. But I warn you—I haven't had time to do laundry in weeks."

"Gross," Molly said.

"Hey, Moll, you're there?"

She moved in front of the webcam so Braden could see her. "Yeah. What's up?"

"Wade Johnson was asking about you."

"Who?"

Braden chuckled. "The lady killer from Langley."

"Wait—the dude from the range?" Molly groaned. "Why was he asking about me?"

"Seems you made quite the impression on him."

"Well, he made an impression on me too—a really bad one."

"I told him you weren't the type to break the rules and date another agent, but that didn't seem to faze him."

Molly nodded, keeping her face and voice neutral. "And if I *were* to break the rules, it wouldn't be for him."

"I'm glad to hear that, Molly." Agent Blevins sounded amused. "So, let's get back on topic here. Braden, head out to Omni tomorrow. Jack, keep working on that footage. I know you've already been working on it, but see what else you can do. Molly, you have a floral shop to open in the morning."

"That's right, sir." She pasted on a bright smile. "And I'll be ready." She hoped that was true.

"Get a good night's sleep then, and let's hit it hard again in the morning. Good night." Agent Blevins clicked off his webcam, and Braden followed suit. Jack didn't move for a moment, staring at the blank screen.

"You should finish your dinner." Molly handed him his sandwich.

"Oh, yeah." He took it without really looking at it.

"So, are you going to bed or what?"

"I'm going to keep working on this footage. I checked all the wiring and physical stuff while we were at the shop, and now I just need to attack it from this angle."

"I thought it *had* been attacked."

"It has. But I'm going after it again."

Molly stayed up and read while Jack worked, her attention wandering from time to time. She had thought that staying near him might show some support and unity, but she could tell he was in his own little world and didn't even know she was there. Deciding to follow Agent Blevins' advice, she finally closed her book and went to bed.

THIRTEEN

Molly groaned as the ringing of the telephone woke her. She hadn't slept much the night before, her worry about Jack blending with her worry about the shop's grand opening, and topping it all off with John Ferguson's murder. She was in no way ready for morning.

"Hello?" she mumbled into the receiver.

"Hello, Sister Bennett? My name is Amy Peterson, and I'm in your new ward. Did I wake you up?"

What an obnoxious question. "Um, no," Molly said. She pressed her thumb to the mouthpiece to muffle it and cleared her throat a few times, thinking that might help her sound more awake. "No, I've been up for hours."

"So you're an early bird just like me! Maybe you'd like to start walking with me. I go at five o'clock every morning."

"I'll definitely think about that." Molly stifled a yawn. The only time she would ever go walking at five o'clock was if there was a bad guy at the other end of that walk and it was her job to catch him.

"Well, let me tell you why I'm calling. I'm in charge of the next Relief Society dinner, which is a week from today, and I wondered if you could make a JELL-O salad. I'm sure you're anxious to get involved and start serving in any way you can."

Molly had to think about that for a minute. How many ways were there to serve? Well, she'd probably serve JELL-O with a big spoon, unless it was the kind in a pan, and then she'd use a spatula. "Sure, I can do that," she said, trusting she'd figure it all out later, after more sleep. "Next Wednesday?"

"Oh, you're a doll! Be at the church a little before six, and don't forget to write your name on the bowl. Thank you!"

Amy said goodbye and hung up. Molly rolled over and tried to go back to sleep, but couldn't. She was too confused. Why would she write her name on her bowl, and why did every conversation she had with a Mormon leave her feeling so lost?

"Tony says he has no idea why John Ferguson was killed," Agent Blevins reported when Jack and Molly called in after breakfast. "We're in the dark on this one until Scarlotti makes contact with you."

"I'm stuck on motive," Jack said. "Why would one of the dons order a hit so early in our negotiations? Nothing has happened yet. We haven't met up with Fabiano, and John was just a handyman with no ties to either group. This isn't sitting right with me."

Molly shook her head. Yesterday Jack had been ready to blame everything on Scarlotti and call it good.

"It's not sitting right with me either," Agent Blevins said. "We need to expand our thinking. It's more likely all the time that we have a different culprit altogether, one not connected to either organization."

Now that Jack was looking at things from different angles, Molly was ready to play the devil's advocate, if you could do that and pretend to be Mormon simultaneously. "But what are the odds of that? Someone just happens to commit murder on our premises while we're conducting an investigation, and it's not related at all? That's not sitting right with *me.* You've got to remember, John was shot in the heart through his back. That's Scarlotti's signature."

"But why would John be so important to Scarlotti that he would come down to the shop personally to carry out the hit?" Jack raked his hand through his hair, and Molly wondered if he was going to have any hair left if he kept it up. "We've run a deep background check on John, and I've never seen someone so clean. This dude has never even run a red light."

"Maybe he's so clean because someone *wiped* him clean. I think the complete lack of any traffic violation is suspicious." Molly said. "Everyone speeds—er, once in a while." Her cheeks grew warm. "Except me, Agent Blevins. I never speed. At all."

"Of course you don't, Molly." His voice sounded like a smile. "I never mistook you for a speeder."

"Thank you, sir," she replied, deciding not to look at Jack.

"Well, speaking of not speeding, you've got a shop to open pretty soon," Agent Blevins said. "I'll leave you to it."

He hung up, and Molly glanced at her watch.

"Yikes—we need to hurry." She grabbed her purse and keys, then paused. "So, tell me I can do this."

Jack met her eyes. "You can do this. And then we'll go shoot something. Okay?"

She grinned. "Okay."

As part of the shop's grand-opening celebration, Jack and Molly were offering a free carnation to the first hundred people who came in. At first Molly hadn't been sure there *were* one hundred people in Omni, but of course she'd realized how silly that was. She filled up buckets with carnations in every color available and placed them in rows in front of the cooler, where everyone could see them and hopefully be enticed to buy more.

The shop was scheduled to open at ten, and as the minute hand crept around the face of the large, decorative clock on the wall, Molly took a few deep breaths. They had announced their opening on the marquee outside and placed an ad in the *Omni Oracle*—would that be enough to draw a crowd? She shouldn't have worried. By five minutes to the hour, the sidewalk was already filled with people lining up to come in. She hadn't thought a floral shop would be such an exciting place to hang out on a weekday morning.

"Welcome to Omni!" A fluttery little woman dressed in georgette was the first through the door, and she gathered Molly up into a hug that smelled of lavender. "My name is Leticia, and I run My Fair Lady, Omni's only fancy dress shop. We should partner up and do weddings together!"

Then came Amy Day, catering. Then came Ruby and Dorothy, owners of Dorothy's Ruby Slippers. These were solid business contacts, ones Molly was glad to make. They would lend more credibility to her cover. What surprised her was the number of people who showed up with casseroles in hand, welcoming her and Jack to the neighborhood, and the invitations to dinner at the homes of complete strangers. She felt welcomed and bombarded all at the same time, and wasn't quite sure how to absorb it.

She slid the casseroles onto the shelves at the back of the walk-in cooler, glad to see that at least half of them were topped with cheese. She was definitely in a cheese mood. Then she returned to the onslaught.

People streamed in, some pushing toddlers in strollers, and others stopping by on their lunch breaks, still clutching their briefcases. Molly was grateful Tansy had volunteered to help—the place was crawling with people, and she couldn't possibly have managed it alone. Ryan was kept busy enough as it was, just ringing people up. Jack stayed in the background, so as not to ruin his tough-guy image—they thought Fabiano might use this opportunity to send a spy into the shop to check them out, and they wanted to give the right impression from the start.

"I never dreamed so many people would want a free carnation." Molly wiped her forehead with her sleeve and removed another empty bucket from the display area. They'd stopped counting around noon and were now just giving a flower to each person who came in, figuring it was good for business.

"Oh, they're not here for the carnations. They're curious about you." Tansy plopped on the stool. They'd only had a few lulls in the traffic all day and were taking whatever opportunities they were given to sit down.

"About me?"

"You and Jason."

"But why?"

"Think about it this way. You're new in town, in a town that rarely gets anything new. You had a murder committed right here in the shop, and so of course people want to come check out the scene of the crime. It's quite a scandal, you know. We all knew John Ferguson, and we never have murders here."

Molly remembered the police saying something like that. "True."

"And I'm sure some of the women are coming in just to check out Jason."

"What?" Molly nearly dropped the spool of ribbon she was holding.

"He's a very good-looking man," Tansy said casually. "And word spreads."

"Word spreads that my husband is a good-looking man?" Molly was incredulous.

"Word spreads about everything."

Ryan came in the back door, his arms full of sacks. "Here's lunch," he announced. Molly stepped forward and took his load from him. "And here's your change." He set a crumpled dollar bill and a couple of pennies on the counter.

"Thanks, Ryan. I know you'd probably rather not play errand boy, but we just haven't had a minute to eat."

"No worries," he said easily. "I'll go sweep out the cooler now." He turned to leave the work area, but paused as he passed the hole in the wall. Molly wondered if she imagined the shudder she saw go through him.

Jack came into the work area from the wedding consultation room, where he'd been holed up with his laptop. He would much rather be downstairs in the command center, but he couldn't very well be disappearing down there with Ryan and Tansy in the shop.

"Oh, good. Lunch." He grabbed a sandwich out of one sack. "Where are these from?"

"Sammy's," Tansy said. "It's a local place just down Main Street aways. Best subs in the world, in my opinion."

Jack took a bite. "This is really good. I'm going to take it with me back in the other room."

"Any luck?" Molly asked.

"Some, but not enough."

Sounded like he'd want to talk to her later. Molly nodded, then unwrapped her own sandwich. She was just about to dive in when the bell on the front door jingled and another customer walked in, followed by two more. She sighed. Lunch would have to wait.

Molly knew him as soon as she saw him. He wasn't dressed any differently from the other customers—in fact, he blended in perfectly. He also wasn't *acting* any differently from the other customers—he seemed normal in every way. But an FBI agent gets a sense, a knowing, after so many years on the job, and when her eyes fell on this particular customer, she knew he was Fabiano's contact.

He approached the counter and leaned on it. "Welcome to Omni. You have very beautiful flowers."

"Thanks," Molly replied. "I see you got your free carnation."

"I did. Your young man over there was very helpful." He nodded toward Ryan, who was organizing the remaining blooms in fresh water. "I wonder if you deliver. My girlfriend has a birthday next week."

"We do deliver. What would you like?"

"I'll come back in a few days when you aren't so busy. Thanks." He turned and left, leaving Molly a little disappointed. The code words hadn't been given, and she wondered if her instincts were off. The murder had distracted them from the real reason they were in Omni, and she was anxious to get back to it.

“I think that was a very successful grand opening.” Molly scooped another chicken enchilada out of a casserole dish. She couldn’t remember which kindly person had brought which meal, but she’d have to figure it out and shower this person with praise. Her taste buds were in cheesy heaven.

“It did go well.” Jack seemed preoccupied, and she knew why. Braden was scheduled to show up any minute, and when he did, Jack would be sharing what he’d found—or what he hadn’t found.

“Want some water?” she asked him.

“Sure.”

She grabbed two cups and filled them, then returned to the table. “We sold six of the arrangements from the cooler, and one was even mine.”

“That’s great. I’m really proud of you, Molly.”

His words were kind, but his tone was far away. A minute later when a knock came at the door, he sprang to answer it, and Molly had confirmation that until he talked to Braden, Jack was going to be on another planet.

She stood and walked over to the wall. Her wedding picture had come in the mail, and Jack found a nice frame for it and hung it between the two bookcases. How had he managed to find the time to do that when he hadn’t even made it to the grocery store? Maybe that blank spot on the wall had been bothering him more than she realized.

“Hey, Molly.” Braden’s voice came from behind her, and Molly turned to greet their visitor.

“Hey,” she replied, pulling her attention back to the present.

"The lab results are all in," Braden reported, "and they were very interesting. For starters, it's highly unlikely that John Ferguson was involved in any way with those drugs. He had no drugs in his system, on his hands, or in his lungs. If he was a dealer, he would have handled the stuff, breathed it while transporting—something. And he wasn't a user—the medical examiner said they'd never seen anyone with such a healthy liver, and the tox screen would probably be clean."

"Makes me wonder what Molly's liver would look like under a microscope," Jack said. "All that coffee she drinks."

"All that coffee I *used* to drink," she corrected. "It's been two days since I've had any, and I'll thank you to stop reminding me."

"Noted." Jack looked at Braden again. "If they're moving sealed packages from one place to another, there wouldn't be so much residue. You saw how much I pulled out on that plastic sack, and still left some behind for the police."

"That's true—not every dealer will have those traces on them. But enough of them do that we have to take that into account," Braden replied. "But there's this. The powder was loose in the hole—it wasn't bagged. If he put it there, he'd have residue on him. And if he was a dealer, but not a user, the powder wouldn't have been loose. We have two scenarios—he was a user and had an open bag on his person, or the drugs were already in the hole when he got there."

"And he probably wasn't a user, based on what the ME said, and he had no powder on his hands, so that pretty much eliminates all possibilities but one," Molly said. "John did not put the drugs into the hole, and therefore they were there when he got there."

"It sounds to me like we've got our motive for the murder," Jack said.

"So John goes into the shop to fix the wall, stumbles across a batch of cocaine hidden there, and gets shot," Molly surmised. She still couldn't understand why the powder was loose. Cocaine was expensive. No dealer or user would have left the package open even the slightest bit. That kind of waste would cut into the profit margin.

"That makes sense to me," Braden said. "Someone with regular access to the shop must have placed the drugs in the wall as a drop-off point. Jack, how are you coming on that footage from the security cameras?"

"Not good. I've isolated that portion of the tape, magnified it, and slowed it way down, and all I'm getting is a shadow. It doesn't even look human, necessarily—and no, Molly, I'm not suggesting this was some kind of alien invasion. I'm just saying that I'm still working on it."

"I wasn't going to suggest aliens," she protested. "Aliens are so cliché. As are zombies."

Jack ignored her. "I'm going to break down the film pixel by pixel and see if I can't find anything to work with. A shoe, a hand—at this point, I'd even take a fingernail."

"Whoever did this must have known the layout of the shop really well," Braden said. "Keep that in mind as you're profiling. And I'd like to head down to the shop and check out everything there."

"Of course."

"Braden, are you hungry?" Molly asked. "We have some chicken enchiladas here."

"I'd love one. Thanks."

He dug in while Jack pulled the security film footage back up on the screen.

"That's the magnification of the shadow?" Molly wondered aloud.

"Yeah. I'm going to break it down even further now." Jack reached out to touch a button on the keyboard, but she stopped him.

"What if that's not a shadow? What if the person was wearing black, and that's actually a picture of them?"

Jack studied the screen. "It's possible. I'll keep that in mind." Ten seconds later he was far, far away in computer-geek land, with Braden joining him on that journey. Molly took the rest of her dinner into her room and sat on the bed, then turned on her own laptop. She might as well work on her next assignment—figuring out how to make a JELL-O salad.

FOURTEEN

Molly studied the list in her hand. She'd gone online to find a recipe for JELL-O salad and had found any number of variations—some of them downright disturbing. Lettuce? Carrots? She hoped she'd chosen the right one, a much more reasonable-sounding concoction containing pineapple, and figured that by shopping for it nearly a week in advance, she wouldn't have any excuse to bow out at the last second. She grabbed a cart from the long line at the grocery store and began pushing it up and down the aisles, thinking that while she was there, she might as well also pick up some food for the house. At this rate, Jack was never going to get the time.

She threw a few things into her cart and rounded a corner, surprised to see Ida Mae Gilmore standing there, her own basket empty.

"Sarah," Ida Mae said warmly. "How are you doing, dear?"

"Truth is, I'm a little confused." Molly parked her cart on the side of the aisle and handed Ida Mae her list. "Do I really want to get walnuts to go with the green JELL-O? That just seems a little odd."

"Well, JELL-O *is* a little odd, dear," Ida Mae said. "And no one really likes it anyway, so it doesn't matter if you put walnuts in it or not."

"But if no one likes it, why do you make it?"

"It's a Mormon tradition. I don't think we'd know what to do with ourselves if we didn't serve at least one JELL-O."

"Is that in your scriptures somewhere?"

"No, but it might as well be." Ida Mae looked down into Molly's cart. "Um, dear, no one taught you how to shop like a Mormon, did they?"

Molly followed Ida Mae's gaze. "Is something wrong?"

"Yes and no. I mean, you're getting food, and that's good . . ." Ida Mae's voice trailed off. "Let me show you a few things. What did you need to get next?"

Molly studied her list. "Bread."

They pushed their carts over to the bread aisle, and Molly reached for a loaf.

Ida Mae coughed.

"I shouldn't get this kind?"

"There's a process." Ida Mae stood back and surveyed the shelf. "First, you look around to see where the sale items are. Then you take into account how many slices come in each loaf, and how much you'd be paying per slice. Then you stand here, and you hem and haw." Ida

Mae paused, then commanded, "Look thoughtful." Molly pasted her best thoughtful look on her face. "Very good. Now, look at your list, and look back at the shelf. Then grab the loaf."

Molly followed the procedure, then placed the bread in the corner of her cart. "I have to go through all that just to buy a loaf of bread?"

"Yes. Now, what's next?"

"Milk."

Over in the dairy section, Molly headed into the thoughtful hemming-and-hawing routine, but Ida Mae stopped her. "Just get the store brand," she said. "I noticed you've got almost nothing but name brands in your cart, and while technically there's nothing wrong with that, you really should start heading for more store brands."

"Why? Oh, let me guess—it's the Mormon way."

"And it's more frugal." Ida Mae put a jug of milk in her own cart as well. "Most store brands and name brands are exactly the same, so you're better off getting the store brand. Except for that!"

Her exclamation nearly made Molly drop the item she was holding. "Why? What's the matter?"

"Never buy that store brand," Ida Mae said. "It all tastes like dog food."

Molly replaced the item. "So, I should buy the store brand, except for when it tastes like dog food. And then I can buy the name brand."

"Exactly." Ida Mae beamed.

"But how do I know which items taste like dog food, and which are fine?"

"A lot of trial and error. And suffering," Ida Mae said. "We do a lot of suffering."

They grabbed a few more things and then walked toward the check-out stand, Ida Mae now satisfied that Molly had everything she needed to make a respectable green JELL-O and even possibly keep from starving to death in the meantime.

"I'm glad I ran into you," Molly told her. "Thanks for your help."

"Well, to be honest, our meeting wasn't exactly coincidental." Ida Mae fidgeted with the strap of her purse. "Jason called me."

"He called you?" Molly looked down at her hands. "What did he say?"

"Just that you were going shopping, and would I please help. There was something in his tone of voice that made me think it was an emergency. I'm glad I came—we clearly averted a disaster here."

Molly shook her head as she loaded the groceries into her car. *It's a sad, sad day when your own husband has to call in reinforcements when you go to the grocery store.*

Molly's dreams that night were a montage of JELL-O salads, crazed drug dealers, and roses with thorny teeth chasing her around the floral shop. She woke up early and stared into the predawn grayness, wondering what was bothering her. Then it came to her. She got out of bed and stumbled into the living room on half-asleep legs, finding Jack right where she'd left him, staring at his laptop. Braden hadn't uncovered anything new and had gone home, leaving Jack a ball of nerves.

"I guess the renovations didn't affect this wall, so the FBI didn't know about the drugs when they moved in here," she said.

Jack didn't reply, but tapped a few keys on his laptop and turned it toward her. It was an e-mail he'd sent to Braden just an hour before, asking that very question.

"Great partners think alike." Molly sat down next to Jack, resisting the urge to brush his hair off his forehead. "Aren't you going to bed?"

"Maybe I'll take a nap before the shop opens." He glanced at his watch. "You're up early."

"Another nightmare about flowers. I wonder if I'll ever stop having them."

Jack exhaled and closed his laptop. "I hate to say it, but I've done everything I can with these tapes. There's nothing here to find."

"But how can there be nothing?"

"I don't know. It doesn't make sense to me either—no one's so good that they don't leave any traces at all. But we're not giving up, if that's what you're worried about. We'll just have to get a little more creative."

"What do you mean?"

"Agent Blevins wanted us to leave the investigation to the locals, but the police aren't making much headway. I don't imagine it would hurt anything too badly if we asked a few questions."

Molly was shocked. Never in all her years of knowing Jack had he ever suggested doing something that wasn't completely sanctioned by Agent Blevins. Jack was the most law-abiding, rule-keeping, stick-in-the-proverbial-mud FBI agent she'd ever met. He needed her spontaneity to keep balance in the universe. And now, he was the one to suggest they investigate? It seemed unnatural.

She decided she shouldn't look too excited, though. That might make him rethink everything. "I guess we could ask a few questions," she said, forcing a note of doubt into her voice. "But only a few."

"And in case you're wondering, I already cleared it with Blevins."

Oh. Here she'd thought Jack was going out on his own a little bit—he'd certainly made it sound that way. It was disappointing to learn he wasn't. She should concentrate on the important part, though: they would get to investigate. That made her feel better about life in general, like her hands weren't tied anymore.

"If the police are hitting the same roadblocks we are, I'm not surprised they're floundering." Jack stretched. "Okay, I'm going to take a nap. Wake me up about a half hour before you leave."

"Okay." Molly watched as he slumped over on the couch. It must be driving him crazy that he couldn't get any information off those tapes—things like this usually just opened right up for him, like he held the magic key.

The phone rang as soon as Jack and Molly walked into the shop. "Omni Orchids," she answered.

"This is Danyelle Ferguson. May I come in and meet with you?"

Molly froze. Ferguson—this must be John Ferguson's wife. Molly wasn't sure how to reply. She'd always struggled with tact, knowing the right things to say, so she'd probably bungle this. "Sure. What time?"

"In about an hour?" Danyelle suggested.

"Perfect."

When the bell on the door rang and the woman entered the shop, Molly took a deep breath and said, "Mrs. Ferguson, please sit down." She indicated the most comfortable chair in the wedding and funeral consultation area. It was awkward, coming face-to-face with the wife of the man who had been murdered not thirty feet away.

"Call me Danyelle." The woman sat and tucked her purse under her chair. "Thank you for agreeing to meet with me."

"Of course. What can I do for you?"

"I need a casket spray, and something nice on an easel."

Molly blinked. "You'd like to order flowers?"

"This is a floral shop, right?"

"Um, yes. I just thought you wanted to discuss what happened or something. Yell at me, or . . ."

Danyelle smiled. "I know this wasn't your fault. I've met with the police and they walked me through all the evidence—well, as much as they could—and I don't blame you in the slightest."

Molly exhaled. "Can we at least donate your flowers? I can't even think about letting you pay for them."

"John was always the type who looked ahead. He bought funeral packages for the two of us a good ten years ago. The flowers, the plot—everything is paid for. You'll get a check from the funeral home, and you're not to worry about it." Danyelle held up a hand when Molly began to protest. "It's hard starting up a new business. You and Jason can't give away your services or you'll never turn a profit."

She was right—Molly needed to think more like a new business owner and less like an undercover FBI agent who really didn't have a stake in the success of the shop. Both personas had a heart, though, and she still felt bad. If Danyelle was going to insist on paying, Molly would bill her at a steep discount.

"Now, show me through this book," Danyelle said.

Molly slid the full-color sample book closer, and they spent the next several minutes looking at the arrangements on each page. For a widow, Danyelle was doing remarkably well, tearing up only when the final selections were made. "He would love these," she said, touching the pictures. "Yes, these are the ones I want."

Molly handed her a tissue, then sat and gave her a moment to collect herself as the tears flowed. "Don't worry about me," Danyelle said after a moment. "I miss him, but thank goodness for the gospel."

Molly searched her memory banks—ah, that's right. Mormons believed that upon death, the spirit left the body and returned to heaven rather than ceasing to exist. That was a very nice thought, and she imagined it would be comforting to a new widow. "Yes, thank goodness," she echoed. "Now, when is the funeral?"

"The police say we can hold the services on Wednesday morning, with a viewing on Tuesday night. Everything should be wrapped up by then."

"That seems fairly quick," Molly said. The police would have to release the body to the funeral home before the arrangements could be made, and it sounded like they'd done all the requisite forensics testing. Had they found what they needed?

"Yes. I'm glad there wasn't more of a delay." Danyelle rose from her chair after collecting her purse. "The viewing will be at six on Tuesday. Can you have the flowers at the funeral home by four?"

"Of course." Molly kept a sympathetic smile on her face until Danyelle left the shop, and then she darted for the phone, pure panic racing through her body. "Um, Tansy? Listen, I'm going to need a lot of help . . ."

Now that the decision had been made to let Jack and Molly investigate, she was raring to go. There was a problem, however, that might slow down the process. She was Sarah Bennett now, not an FBI agent, and she couldn't flash her ID and demand answers of anyone she wished to question. She'd have to be a lot more subtle and start with the people in Omni she knew, and that list was pretty short.

Molly perched on a stool near the counter at the Hard Book Café and watched as Melissa poured her two cups of hot chocolate to go.

"I just can't get over it," Molly said truthfully. "I've never had someone murdered in my shop before."

"I can't imagine." Melissa put lids on the cups and placed them on the counter, then turned to bag the cinnamon rolls Molly had ordered. "You've handled it really well."

"Not as well as I would like." Molly's idea of handling something involved making an arrest—high-speed car chase optional. "Did you know John Ferguson well?"

"I knew him, but I wouldn't say really well," Melissa replied. "He came in about once a week and we'd chat about paint or something like that. He bought some interior-decorating magazines and a *National Geographic* for Roger from time to time, but mainly he picked up breakfast."

"I met John's wife this morning. She seems nice."

Melissa set the bag of cinnamon rolls next to the hot chocolate and sighed. "She and I went to high school together. We were pretty good friends and we've stayed in touch, even though we aren't as close anymore. I should go over and see her, take her some treats or something. It's just a little awkward because we had a . . . well, not a fight, exactly, but a disagreement."

Molly toyed with the fold on top of the bag, wondering how deeply she could pry. Melissa inadvertently ended her dilemma by continuing to talk without extra encouragement.

"She and John dated all through high school, and he'd gotten into some trouble. Just a little bit, mind you—he never was the kind to break the rules."

That sounded like Jack, come to think of it.

"Well, he made some friends he shouldn't have made—they were involved with drugs, and I was worried. I didn't think Danyelle should keep seeing him, not until he got rid of those friends. But she didn't listen and ended up marrying him. We stayed friends, but not like we had been."

Molly thought it over for a second. Not one shred of evidence had been found to suggest John was involved in drugs. His record had been clean, and that by itself seemed suspicious. But what if he had friends who dealt drugs, and they'd asked him to help them out just for old time's sake?

"She made some good choices for the funeral flowers," Molly said, just to fill in the silence.

"I'm sure she did. She always had a flair for that kind of thing."

Melissa moved to the end of the counter to help someone else, and Molly popped the lid off her cup and took a sip. Just who were these friends of John Ferguson's, and how involved had they been in his life recently?

FIFTEEN

The previous Saturday, the shop had been really busy. Maybe that's because it was their first weekend in business, and everyone was curious. Or the people who couldn't make it to the Wednesday grand opening because of work had come on the weekend instead. Molly had geared herself up for another hectic Saturday, but it was eleven forty-five and not one customer had come in or called. What was even more strange, when she went outside to change the sign in front, she didn't see any cars on the road or a single person milling around. It was as though everyone had vanished. She didn't believe in the Rapture, but for one split second, she wondered.

A few minutes after noon, the phone rang, and Molly startled. She hadn't expected the loud ring after two hours of dead silence. Then customers began to come in, and she was kept pretty busy right up until a quarter to two, when everything went totally, completely still again.

Jack came up from the control room. "What's up?"

"Absolutely nothing," she muttered. "I could be painting my nails and watching them dry right now and having more fun than what I'm doing. I'm bringing a book next time."

Jack held up his laptop. "Agent Blevins just e-mailed the police file on the John Ferguson case. And there's a note here—the police still don't know we're FBI, so we shouldn't let them know we have this file. They released it only to Agent Blevins."

"Great. Now we can see what they've figured out—or not figured out."

"I'll get started on this right now. Wanna help?"

Molly sighed. "No, I'd better make some stupid flowers for the cooler. I was procrastinating, but my boredom has driven me to a new realization of my duty. You can fill me in later."

Four o'clock came around, and a few minutes later, the shop was filled with customers again. Molly couldn't explain it. Nothing at all between ten and noon, decent flow between noon and two, and then nothing between two and four. It was so strange.

Ida Mae popped by a little while later, and Molly told her about the strange phenomenon. Ida Mae laughed long and hard, then wiped tears from her eyes. "You know, I never stopped to think about it from a business perspective, but yes, I imagine that was very strange indeed."

"What? What's going on?"

"It's general conference weekend. That means that instead of going to church tomorrow, we'll watch meetings on television. And the first sessions are today, so

I imagine everyone was watching them instead of doing their shopping."

"So that's why this place looked like a ghost town when I went outside?"

"Exactly. And it's just something we always do, so it never occurred to me that it would seem odd to someone from out of town."

Molly was happy to have an explanation, but then her brain looped back around to a key point. "Did you say there's no church tomorrow?"

"I did say that. But there's a meeting for the men tonight at the church building, and it would be nice if Jason came. George could swing by and pick him up, if that would be less awkward."

"Um, sure. That would probably work out."

Jack wasn't overly thrilled to hear that he needed to attend a meeting on a Saturday night, but he was more than delighted that there wasn't any church the next day, so he went without a fuss. And the next morning, when he and Molly slept in and stayed in their jammies all day, they were both very happy indeed.

Things became very awkward for Molly on Monday when the flower orders started coming in for John Ferguson's funeral. She'd already asked Tansy to help out—being the only florist in town, it wasn't hard to figure out that Omni Orchids would be handling the event—but knowing it and actually moving through the steps were two different things. Molly wrote down the messages for the cards, touched by the kind words and wishing with all her heart that this seemingly good man had not been murdered here, in her shop—that he could be out boating or picnicking with his family, alive and well.

She was wrestling with a particularly ornery stem of baby's breath when Roger Ferguson walked in. His gait was slow and his head bowed, the total opposite of his demeanor when she'd first met him.

"I'd like to patch up that hole in the wall," he said by way of greeting.

"You don't have to do that. We can call someone else. We should have done it already." Molly put down her arrangement and walked around the counter to where he stood. "Please don't worry about it."

"A Ferguson never leaves a job undone. And if John can't do it, well . . ." Roger shrugged. "I will."

Molly opened her mouth to protest again, then realized as she looked at him that he needed to do this for his brother. Maybe it was some kind of saying-goodbye ritual.

"All right. That would be fine."

Roger nodded. "I'll get my things from the truck."

A few minutes later, the corner of the workroom was filled with a bucket of Spackle, a little pail of paint, and a few other tools and gizmos Molly couldn't call by name. Roger worked quickly, filling in the hole with a replacement brick he'd found somewhere and spackling it all around, and then adding a good thick layer of quick-drying mortar. After taking a break while the mortar firmed up, he painted it until it matched the rest of the wall.

"I stuck it in there good and tight. It's not going anywhere now," he explained.

"Thank you," Molly said. "What do I owe you?"

"Not one penny. Not one blessed penny. This was for John."

Roger gathered up his things and shuffled out the door, leaving her speechless.

The man came back that afternoon, the one Molly was sure was their mob contact. He walked up to the counter shortly after Thelma Brown placed an order for three yellow roses in a bud vase to be delivered to her daughter at her new office on her first day of work. He smelled of expensive cologne, and Molly knew she'd pegged him right the first time. This was their guy.

"Hello again," she said. "Girlfriend's birthday, right?"

"You have a great memory." He flashed her a smile. "I'd like to send her eighteen red tulips in a crystal vase, delivered around noon on Friday."

"Noon on Friday," Molly repeated as she wrote it down on an order form for the sake of appearance.

"Yes."

"I'm sure we can do that. Let me talk to the owner. He'll be able to tell you for sure." Molly walked into the wedding consultation area. "Honey, can we deliver eighteen red tulips in a vase next Friday?"

Jack rose from the table and squared his shoulders. She loved watching him undercover—he stepped in and out of roles so effortlessly, it was almost as if he had a split personality. His jawline became harder and more pronounced, his eyes became more steely—and all in the amount of time it took for him to round the corner and approach the counter.

"Eighteen red tulips delivered?"

The man turned at the sound of Jack's voice. "That's right."

"I'm sure we can do that."

Jack motioned to the other room, and the man followed him to the consultation tables. Molly was itching to wander in there too, but her role demanded that she stay where she was and work on the flowers. She was Joe Baker's girlfriend and his flower-making assistant, not his partner.

She took a phone order for six peach roses wrapped in cellophane to be picked up in fifteen minutes, and kept herself busy arranging the ferns just so. The ribbon actually cooperated this time, and the customer seemed pleased. Once the door had closed again, Molly inhaled sharply and sat on the stool, wondering how long Jack's meeting was going to take. The suspense might not kill her, but it was definitely committing attempted murder.

"Babe, come in here," Jack called a moment later.

She hopped off the stool and walked into the other room. "Yeah?"

"How would you like to go to a party?"

"A party? I'd love it. It's so boring in this tiny little town." She trailed her fingernails along Jack's shoulder.

"Sean here has invited us to a cocktail party this Friday night."

Molly squealed—just a little. She wasn't a natural squealer, and forcing it would be even more unnatural. "Thank you! I'm dying to have some real fun."

"We'll see that you get your wish." Sean rose from his chair, shook Jack's hand, and strode out of the shop.

Molly plunked down in the recently vacated chair. "So? Tell me everything."

"He didn't say much about the organization—just that Fabiano was looking forward to meeting me."

"Sean seemed nice enough, for a mobster."

"Yeah, he was very cordial. Asked me how we were settling in, stuff like that." Jack stretched his arms over his head. "I'm starved. Want me to go grab something?"

Her stomach growled in reply. "That would be great."

"Okay, I'll be right back."

Ryan arrived while Jack was gone. He stopped and looked at the wall for a long moment. Molly tried to guess how he was feeling, but he was inscrutable.

"Turned out pretty well, didn't it? Roger came in and fixed it," Molly said.

"Yeah. It looks like new." Ryan grabbed the broom and began to sweep out the cooler. He seemed subdued—not that he was ever brimming with joy, but he didn't even whistle when he thought she couldn't hear him, like he usually did.

"Everything okay, Ryan?" she asked when he emerged from the cooler.

"Yeah, I'm fine."

That was a lie if ever one had been uttered. "So, you graduated last year, right?"

"Yeah."

This was going nowhere fast. "What do you like to do on the weekends?"

"Hang out. Play video games."

"Oh, yeah? Which ones?"

"World of Warcraft, mostly."

"No kidding. I love that game."

Ryan turned to her with a look of shock. "You do?"

Molly nodded. "No lie. I don't have time to play it as often as I want, but I have a level 85 druid. I spec'd her as resto. Whenever my guild needs healz, they come to me."

"Cool." It was still a one-word answer, but Ryan was looking at her with begrudging admiration, and Molly figured that was a small victory.

"So, you say you never met John Ferguson, right? We're doing his funeral flowers tomorrow."

"He lived in my neighborhood and I knew who he was, but we never, like, talked or anything. I doubt he knew my name."

"Hmm. Well, I think his flowers will turn out nicely. The shipment will be here first thing tomorrow, and I'd like you to come in and get them unpacked."

"Okay."

Apparently Ryan had used up his word-count allowance with that super-huge speech he'd made. Molly decided she'd persecuted him enough for one day and let him get on with his job list while she took inventory in the cooler. She'd never admit it, but she was actually kind of starting to like some aspects of her job.

SIXTEEN

"This is going to be so much fun!" Tansy said when she bustled into the shop at eleven on Tuesday morning, her purse over one arm and a plastic sack filled with Tupperware containers in the other. "I love doing funeral flowers, and I brought lunch."

"You didn't have to do that," Molly replied. "I was going to take us out somewhere."

"Nonsense. You can't live on fast food—you've got to have some home cooking from time to time."

Tansy tucked the food into the back of the cooler, then stepped into the work area. The flowers and greenery she had requested from the floral distributor sat in buckets in the corner. Unpacking them was the last task Molly had given Ryan before sending him home for the day. He already knew she had some unorthodox methods of floral design, but she didn't want him to know she had to bring in a ringer for the big jobs. Tansy had also come in the night before to help with the arrangements ordered by family and friends, and they were lined up in the cooler, ready to go.

"Oh, these are gorgeous." Tansy fingered the huge white roses in the first bucket. "And these greens—they're so *green.*"

Molly wondered what Tansy meant by that—weren't all greens green? But she took a closer look at them. Huh. These did seem to be a little more vibrant, a little richer.

"Maybe they know they're for a funeral, and wanted to look their best." Tansy grabbed an apron from the hook and tied the strings around her ample middle.

Molly didn't know how to reply to that, so she didn't.

For the next hour, she watched with rapt attention while Tansy demonstrated how to put together a casket spray. The foam was set in a plastic holder curved to fit over the top of a casket, and then layers upon layers of leaves and ferns were inserted all around. Danyelle had chosen a spray made only of various types of greens, explaining that John had been the outdoors type, and then asked for a few sprigs of autumn leaves to be used throughout as well. Jack had gone out first thing in the morning on a tromp through the woods near town and found some nice branches.

Tansy gasped when she saw them. "Oh, these are perfect." She tucked the ends of the branches down into the foam as well, and Molly loved the effect. It was masculine, it was outdoorsy, and she wished she had even the tiniest bit of artistic talent. Tansy's creation was going to touch someone's heart, and Molly wanted the ability to do that too. But then she reminded herself Tansy probably couldn't shoot the eye out of a rabid dog at three hundred yards—everyone had their own special talent.

The two women each took an end of the spray and carried it into the large back area of the cooler to wait for delivery. Then Tansy turned to Molly with an excited look on her face and said, "Your turn."

"What?"

"Your turn. You're going to make the easel spray."

"No. No, I'm not." Molly backed up, her hands in front of her. "I'm not going to ruin a funeral—especially not when the man was killed in my own shop."

"You're not going to ruin anything. I'll be right here, and I'll walk you through every step."

"But—"

Tansy put one hand on her hip. "Sarah, if you're going to live here and run this shop and make people believe you are who you say you are, you've got to push yourself. It's not that hard, and you've got to let go of this idea that you can't do it."

These little old ladies were sure perceptive sometimes. "Okay," Molly said after a long moment. "How do we start?"

The hour that followed was one of the most nerve-racking of Molly's life. She remembered a standoff with a gunman holding his four children and wounded ex-wife hostage in their minivan. Molly had kept her rifle trained on him for three solid hours before she was finally able to get off a clean shot and bring the situation to a close. She'd known what she was doing then. She'd been trained, she had backup, the law was on her side, and she had no fear. Well, not until it was over and she cried herself to sleep in Jack's arms. Now she had none of those assurances, and she didn't even have Jack's arms.

"You're doing great," Tansy told her. "Now trim about five inches off this stem and insert the rose here."

If only Molly's hands would stop trembling. She did as she was told and then stepped back. "Now what?"

"Now we're done." Tansy beamed.

"What do you mean, we're done? We can't be done. It's not any good. I mean, it doesn't look like the picture in the book at all."

Tansy picked up the book and looked from the picture to the arrangement, and back again. "I really don't see much difference. What's bothering you?"

Molly peered over Tansy's shoulder and made the same comparison. "Huh. They really do look alike. I guess—I guess I just didn't think I was capable of it."

"That's the whole problem right there. You think too much. It gets you all tied up inside. I do as little thinking as I can—and that's why my blood pressure is so low."

The bell over the door jingled, and Ida Mae and Arlette entered the shop. Molly was a little startled to see them approach from the front of the store—they had been using the back door until now, like good friends, which they were quickly becoming.

"We thought we'd come see if we could lend any moral support," Ida Mae said. "And we brought cookies."

"Thank you," Molly said fervently. "I don't know what it is about this place, but it makes me want chocolate in the worst way."

Ida Mae walked around the easel spray. "These flowers are really beautiful, Tansy."

"Sarah did it. I just helped."

Molly held up a hand in protest. "That is not true. Tansy was more than just a helper—she saved my skin today."

"We just came from the Fergusons'." Arlette settled herself in the chair in the corner. "Please tell us the police are close to catching John's killer."

"I wish I had some good news, but I don't," Molly replied. "The truth is, the killer covered his tracks really well."

"Can't the FBI do something?"

"Actually, Arlette, we have started to investigate. Quietly." Molly put some emphasis on the last word. These ladies hadn't blown her cover yet, but she worried that it was just a matter of time. Despite the impressive number of cases they'd solved on their own, they weren't professionals, and she didn't know if she could trust them to be totally discreet. She wondered, though . . . "Would you three be interested in helping me with a little bit of detective work?"

Tansy looked hurt. "I thought we were already signed up to help you."

"Just tell us what you need," Ida Mae put in. "We know this town better than the backs of our own wrinkled hands."

"Speak for yourself," Arlette retorted. "My hands are not wrinkled."

"And your eyes need to be examined." Ida Mae lifted her chin and turned back to Molly. "What's our first assignment?"

"The police have already talked to all the shop owners up and down the street, but that was a week ago. Sometimes we remember things after the adrenaline rush has subsided. Can you talk to the owners and employees, see if you can find out if they saw or heard anything on the morning of the murder? Carefully, please—don't let them know that you're working for us or trying to help solve the case."

"We are the epitome of discretion," Arlette said.

Ida Mae looked thoughtful for a moment. "Well, I don't know if we're the epitome, but we're pretty darned good. What else?"

"Do you know the Fergusons' neighbors?" Molly asked. "We need to talk to them and find out if John and Danyelle had been fighting lately or had any suspicious-looking visitors."

"We know pretty much everyone in Omni," Arlette said. "That assignment won't be a problem."

"I'm really glad to hear it. I have a feeling the three of you will be able to get information more easily than Jason or I would. We have to stay low key, and I'm worried that if we ask too many questions, people will start to suspect we aren't just here to start a floral shop."

"And people know we're super nosy, so they won't think anything of it if we ask." Tansy added one more piece of fern to a bare spot on the side of the arrangement.

"I already spoke to Melissa Coon next door, but it wouldn't hurt a thing if you talked to her as well," Molly explained. "She said John ran around with a bad crowd in high school."

"Yes, he did." Arlette shook her head. "That boy was practically Roger's undoing."

It was hard to picture the man on the floor of the cooler as a boy—he looked to be in his midthirties—but then again, to Arlette, maybe everything under forty looked young. "What do you mean, Roger's undoing?"

"Roger was the oldest in his family, and there were eight boys. Their father died when Roger was about fourteen, so he became the role model for his brothers. He started his painting and carpentry business right out of high school so his brothers would always have jobs. When John started hanging out with those unsavory characters, Roger worried that his hard work and sacrifices had been for nothing and that he would lose John from the family fold, which would devastate their mother."

Molly had always thought the term "unsavory characters" sounded funny, like someone had taken the characters and stripped them of all their tasty herbs and seasonings. "But John was in here working, wasn't he?"

"Oh, he and Roger made up years ago." Arlette waved her free knitting needle complacently. "But I think Roger was always a little worried that John was just biding his time."

"Had John done anything to make Roger think that?"

"Roger was just being paranoid," Ida Mae said. "Truth is, yes, some of John's friends were involved in drugs and alcohol, but he was never arrested or found to have any illegal substances on his person. It was one of those guilt-by-association things. I don't believe for a minute that John Ferguson was using drugs."

"Roger was probably just worried about their mother," Tansy said. "She's really old now, even older than Ida Mae, and her heart's not very strong. I think Roger just wanted to protect her, and that's why he was scared."

"Probably," Ida Mae said. "Have you met John's mother, Sarah?"

"No, I haven't."

"I imagine it's a terrible thing for a mother to lose a child for any reason, but to a murder . . ." Ida Mae took the lid off the cookie container and set it in the counter. "We can't discuss sad topics without a snack."

Each lady took a cookie and nibbled. Well, nibbling was Molly's intention, but when the rush of cinnamon mixed with chocolate hit her taste buds, she all but inhaled the cookie.

"Wow. What kind of cookie was that?"

"Pumpkin chocolate chip. Haven't you had one before?"

"No. We don't really do much with pumpkins where I'm from, aside from carve them and make pies. But we don't make pies from the ones we've carved. Usually."

"Well, out here, as soon as the fall weather hits, we make pumpkin everything." Ida Mae handed her another cookie. "Pumpkin bread, pumpkin pancakes, pumpkin eggnog . . . "

"And don't forget pumpkin waffles with vanilla ice cream. That's Earl's favorite fall treat," Tansy added.

"I'd ask you for the recipe if I thought I'd be able to use it," Molly said around another mouthful. She didn't know where these cookies had been all her life—they were amazing.

"I'll put you on my emergency cookie list. That way, whenever I bake, you'll be sure to get some."

"Okay. You do that." How could Molly turn down such an incredibly generous offer? It would probably come across as unfriendly or something, and she didn't want to take those kinds of chances.

A glance at the clock told her it was almost three thirty. "Tansy, thank you so, so much for your help. I've got to deliver these to the funeral home now—do you really think they look nice?"

Tansy put her hand on Molly's shoulder. "Sarah, you did a wonderful job. Now stop second-guessing yourself and make this delivery."

The three ladies bustled out of the shop, and a moment later Jack came up from the command center. "Are you ready to do this thing?"

"Not really, but I guess we'd better, huh?"

They loaded everything into the delivery van, careful to wedge foam between the containers to keep them from tipping during the drive. Last, they loaded the casket spray. Molly had a vision of either herself or Jack losing their footing and the entire arrangement flying through the air and coming to land upside down, but they made it without any incidents and everything still looked great when they pulled up in front of the funeral home.

The mortician met them in the hallway and directed them to the viewing room. He'd already set up tables and stands for the flowers, so it was simple to see where they should go. Jack placed the easel spray near the end of the casket. An arrangement with red gladiola that Molly had done herself, with only about a hundred hints from Tansy, looked wonderful on the stand near the door. The casket spray was a masterpiece and suited the earthy wood tones of the casket perfectly, and as Jack and Molly walked out of the building, she felt as though she'd done a good thing in helping John Ferguson's family find some peace in their loss.

Peace, but not closure. That wouldn't come until they caught the murderer, and Molly wasn't about to give up. A glance at the set of Jack's shoulders told her that he was thinking the same thing.

SEVENTEEN

"Hey." Molly came into the living room and sat on the ottoman near Jack's feet. "What are you working on?"

"Just reading over the police file."

"Again? You probably have it memorized by now."

"Just about. But I want to make sure I'm not missing something here." Jack put his laptop down. "I feel like our hands are tied—we're relying on three little old ladies to do our legwork for us."

"I think they'll do a good job. They're going to nose around a bit at the funeral, see what juicy tidbits of gossip they pick up."

Something in her voice must have set off Jack's radar. "While you have to sit and watch them do it, and it's driving you nuts."

"Yeah, pretty much. Sometimes being undercover stinks."

"I agree. So, what time is the funeral, anyway?"

"Eleven. I put a sign on the shop door saying we're closed until one. Oh, and don't forget, I have that Relief Society dinner thing tonight. I'd better get started on the salad." Molly stood up.

"Are you really going to do it yourself? Do you want my help?"

"I think I should learn how. It's good for me."

Jack blinked at her, not speaking.

"I know, I know. Just let me try, okay?"

He shrugged, and Molly went into the kitchen. She had printed the recipe and stuck it to the fridge with a magnet, and now she studied it. Boil water—she could do that. She pulled a saucepan from the cupboard and measured the water into it, then set it on the stove. While it heated, she pulled out the rest of the ingredients. It took her a minute to find some things—she should have paid better attention when Jack showed her around the kitchen. He had seemed to think she'd want to know where things like the colander were kept. She didn't care that they even owned a colander, let alone where it was kept.

"Are you okay in there?" Jack called.

"I'm fine. Why wouldn't I be fine?"

"You've been at it for quite a while, and you keep muttering to yourself."

"It hasn't been that long, and I'm not muttering."

"Yes, you are."

She decided to ignore him. Wait—how long had the water been boiling? A couple of minutes at least, and the pan didn't look as full as it did. She'd probably boiled away enough water that the recipe wouldn't work now. She poured the hot water down the sink and refilled the pan.

"Are you sure you're all right?"

"Do you want to come do this yourself, Jack? Because I'm getting that impression."

"No, it's all right. I think you can do it."

"That tone in your voice says otherwise."

He chuckled. "I was up pretty early, and I'm going to take a nap until the funeral. Maybe you could keep the muttering to a minimum so I can sleep."

The next half hour was a blur. Somewhere between the walnuts and the pineapple, Molly wanted to cry. No, what she really wanted to do was shoot it, but if she couldn't shoot flowers, she probably couldn't shoot JELL-O, either, and she wanted to know who made up these dumb rules.

Then she was faced with a dilemma. Should she put the JELL-O into a bowl or a casserole dish? She didn't have a mold, and she didn't entirely trust those anyway—they looked like sand-castle wannabes, and she didn't think any food that aspired to be a sand castle should be eaten. Finally she settled on a glass casserole dish and poured the mixture evenly into the bottom, although perhaps a small amount sloshed onto the counter. Then she slid the pan into the fridge, thinking she'd done the very best she could, and that all she could do now was hope it was enough.

The funeral was held at the church building rather than the funeral home, and Molly wondered if the mortician had taken care in transporting the flowers. Then she told herself to stop obsessing—the man was a professional and knew what he was doing. Still, she glanced around anxiously and was relieved to see that everything still looked beautiful.

She and Jack wanted to sit somewhere inconspicuous, but the only empty seats were in the middle of the chapel. They sat, and Molly instantly felt a hundred sets of eyes bore into the back of her head. She wished she knew what everyone was thinking—whether they blamed her for John Ferguson's death or if they knew she was a fake and hadn't made all the floral arrangements.

The service was very nice. Molly had only attended a handful of funerals in the past, two of the most notable being those of her grandparents. Her grandfather had died in a car accident when Molly was fourteen, and her grandmother passed away from lung cancer two years ago. Both services were bleak, held for people taken before their time. Molly expected the same note of negativity in the sermons for John, but it wasn't there. Hope underscored the entire meeting, and while people cried, the overall message spoke of a reunion on the other side someday. Molly had no idea what to think of that.

After the casket was wheeled out and the funeral ended, she was surprised at the large number of people who approached her and Jack and offered their condolences that the death had taken place in their shop.

"What an awful welcome to Omni," one woman said.

"Are you two all right? Do you need anything?" another asked.

"We're fine, but thank you," Jack told them over and over until he and Molly escaped to their car.

"That was really something else," she said as she buckled her seatbelt.

"Yeah. Can you believe it? They were asking us if *we're* all right."

The whole service gave Molly an awful lot to think about while she stripped the thorns off roses that afternoon.

She drove to the church building that night with the JELL-O salad on the seat beside her, its faults covered by a generous layer of Cool Whip. Not the fat-free kind—Ida Mae had proclaimed it only one step up from the telestial kingdom, whatever that was.

Molly parked, picked up the salad, and walked toward the building, her knees almost as wobbly as the green goop in the pan she carried. She had no idea what to expect from a gathering of religious women.

"Sarah!" Molly recognized the high-pitched voice as belonging to Amy, the woman who'd called her on the phone and given her this odd assignment in the first place. "Thank you so much for coming. The salad looks delicious!"

Molly forced a smile. "Delicious" was not the word that came to mind when she looked at her concoction.

The ladies in the building bustled around, all calling her by name and congratulating her on the opening of the shop, as well as offering additional condolences about John's death. Molly recognized a few of the women from the Sunday before, some from the funeral, and several who had come to the grand opening of Omni Orchids. She didn't recognize a good third of them, though, and wondered how it was that a town so small could hold so many people. Did Mormons magically duplicate themselves or something, like amoebas?

A woman Molly remembered was the Relief Society president stood and thanked everyone for coming, especially those who had helped with the funeral. It sounded as if the ladies had worked together to feed the family after the service, and that seemed like a sweet thing to do.

After sitting through a lesson that made no sense—something about building gardens off the ground, because gardens *on* the ground aren't good enough—Molly wandered over to the quilting frames. She felt completely out of place and she'd spotted Arlette, a familiar face in a sea of friendly strangers.

"I'm not sure I dare let you touch this quilt." Arlette handed over a needle with yarn threaded through it.

"Oh, come on." Molly glanced around to see that no one was listening. "I'm not totally hopeless. I made a JELL-O salad."

Arlette raised an eyebrow. "That's progress, certainly. Now let's see if you can tie a quilt."

Molly knew she could be a frustrating person. She'd certainly irritated Agent Blevins often enough, and Jack had put up with her for as long as he could. But with all her failings, she had never considered herself capable of giving someone a stroke. As Arlette untangled the yarn that Molly had somehow turned into a big ball of knots,

Molly wondered if perhaps that was exactly what she had done.

"Yarn can be tricky." Arlette took a deep breath. She appeared to be doing yoga in her mind, or some other sort of stress-management trick. Molly didn't know why something as simple as yarn was making her so edgy. She thought Arlette liked yarn.

"You must treat it with respect, and then it will do whatever you ask," Arlette said.

Would it bring me a cup of coffee? For two very uncomfortable seconds, Molly thought she'd said that out loud, but then realized she hadn't and bent her head back to her task.

A half hour later, she gazed with shock at the fabric stretched out below her. There, plain as day, was an entire twelve-inch section of quilt that she, herself, had tied. It hadn't come without a high price. Her fingers were pricked until she felt like she was at the shop wrestling with roses. She'd pulled some batting through the back—which was worse than killing someone, according to Arlette. And she'd created three more knots, which other kindly ladies undid for her—Arlette had given up after the first one. But now, success! Molly had done it!

She reached into her pocket for her cell phone and took a close-up picture of the quilt. She wanted proof, some way to commemorate that yes, she actually was not a total failure in the whole womanhood department. And when she looked up, she thought she saw a little bit of approval in Arlette's eyes.

EIGHTEEN

"There you are." Ida Mae bustled into the shop and plunked her purse down on the counter. "I need to ask you something."

Molly looked up from the wrist corsage she was trying—unsuccessfully—to hot glue onto an elastic bracelet. Tansy had shown her this trick twice, but Molly was no closer now than when she started. "What's up?"

"First off, I'm sorry I missed the Relief Society dinner last night. I was invited to a wedding. Kevin, one of our very dear friends, finally tied the knot with Maren, a girl we met on one of our cases. She's a wonderful girl. Granted, at first we thought she might be a murderer—or rather, a horse killer—but she wasn't, and now she and Kevin are married. It really was a wonderful ceremony."

Molly didn't even try to follow that. She just let Ida Mae's words wash over her and waited to see what settled.

"That's all right. It was a nice dinner, but I'm sure the wedding was nicer."

"I just wanted to be there to show you the ropes, you know?"

"Arlette showed me the yarn." Molly pulled up the picture on her phone. "Can you believe it? I tied that part of the quilt all by myself."

"Very impressive." Ida Mae nodded. "We'll make a Mormon out of you yet. I believe next on the convert agenda is canning."

"Um, maybe we can just consider me partially converted."

Ida Mae laughed. "Well, I'm here for two reasons. First off, I'd like to invite you over for dinner tonight. I feel just terrible that you've been here for two whole weeks and we haven't gotten together yet."

"I'd like that." Molly walked to the doorway that separated the workroom from the consultation room, where Jack was studying the building schematics in relation to the camera angles. Again. "Jason, Ida Mae would like us to come over for dinner tonight. Are we free?"

"Sure. Sounds good."

"The man approves." Molly walked back over to the counter. "Can we bring anything? Preferably something I can pick up ready-made so I don't risk giving you food poisoning?"

"No, not a thing. I'll handle all the food poisoning myself." Ida Mae winked. "We're very casual—just dust the leaves off your shirt and come on over at six."

She waved goodbye over her shoulder as she left, and Molly looked down at her shirt. Yes indeed, some tree-fern fragments clung to the front of it. At least they proved she'd been busy doing actual floral stuff.

Ryan came in a moment later, and rather than grabbing a broom or a bucket and getting to work like he usually did, he hovered for a moment by the cooler door. He didn't say anything, and Molly sensed he felt awkward about something, like he wanted to ask a question or give her some bad news and wasn't sure how to go about it.

"Um," he said after a long moment.

"What's the matter, Ryan?"

"Well, see, I was wondering if I could maybe . . ."

Molly waited, but the kid wasn't talking. She exhaled loudly. "Let me explain how this works. If you spit it out, you'll get it over with faster."

He closed his eyes. "Can I have an advance on my check, and can I work some extra hours to pay for it?" He ran this all together, almost like a new version of "supercalifragilisticexpialidocious," and Molly smiled.

"See? Isn't that better? How much do you need?"

He closed his eyes again, like he didn't want to see her face when he said it. "A hundred dollars?"

"I think that would be all right." She walked over to the register, unlocked it, and withdrew the money in twenty-dollar bills. Ryan stared at them for a moment before shoving them into his pocket.

"Thank you," he stammered. "And I'll work extra hard, I promise."

"I'll hold you to that." As Molly returned to the ever-exciting task of bow making, she wondered if she was setting a bad precedent, but Ryan had been a faithful, if somewhat bland, employee, and she knew he'd work off the advance.

Molly came back inside from changing the sign on the marquee and heard a voice echoing from the workroom. It was Ryan, and it sounded like he was on the phone. She paused, eavesdropping. It was part of her job.

"It's okay. I got the money." Pause. "No, she was cool about it. Everything's going to be fine—just calm down. Okay, I'll call you later. Bye."

Hmm. So Ryan hadn't wanted the money for himself—someone else had been counting on it. There was a note of urgency in his voice as he spoke. The person on the other end didn't just want to go out to dinner and a movie—something a little bigger was at stake. But a hundred dollars wouldn't go very far. Molly wanted to ask Ryan about it, but he'd had a reason for waiting until she was outside to place the call. He was hiding something and would most likely lie if she confronted him. Best to keep an eye on things and see how they played out.

"I'm a little nervous," Molly whispered as she and Jack walked up the steps of the Gilmores' modest redbrick home. "Isn't a bishop kind of like a pope or something?"

"You saw him at church our first Sunday here. Did he seem scary to you?"

"No, he looked kind of like Yoda. But you know how *not* religious I am. I don't want to say something wrong or do something wrong . . ."

"Molly, he knows we're not members. He's not going to have a rigid set of expectations. Besides, he's Ida Mae's husband. Can you picture her married to someone who isn't nice?"

"No, I guess not."

Molly smoothed her skirt while Jack rang the bell. She didn't know why she was so edgy. She bet she could trace it back to her childhood—just about everyone could, right? Maybe there was an overly austere pastor in the small Presbyterian church she'd attended a few times when she was nine. Or she was accidentally locked in a closet with the sacramental wine when she and her mother visited a Catholic service when she was ten. Something had to explain why her knees felt a little spongy now.

Bishop Gilmore threw open the door in welcome just as Molly realized why she was nervous. "Can you read my mind?" she blurted.

The bishop raised an eyebrow. "I'm sorry?"

"I've heard people say that their preachers can read their minds."

"Come in and give me your coats. Ida Mae has warmed up some cider—it's a bit chilly out." He ushered Jack and Molly inside and handed each of them a heavenly smelling drink, then showed them to the couch in the living room.

"And now that you're comfortable, why don't you tell me what you think. *Can* I read your mind?"

While the man who sat before her did resemble Dumbledore in some ways—mostly because they were both very, very old—she didn't think George Gilmore seemed magical in any way. "I would say no," Molly replied after a moment.

"And you would be correct. As I serve the Lord and listen to the Spirit, I'm guided in how best to help people, but no, I can't read your mind." Bishop Gilmore leaned back and studied her with a gleam in his eye. "Were you worried I'd see something embarrassing in there?"

"No! Um, maybe." Molly took another sip. He might not be a mind reader, but he sure was perceptive. She had all kinds of stuff jumbled up in her brain. She imagined it was a pretty dark, confusing place, and she wouldn't want an elderly man to get lost in there.

Ida Mae bustled out of the kitchen, an apron tied over her purple pantsuit. "I'm so glad you could make it," she said genially. "I had a small emergency in the kitchen or I would have greeted you sooner."

"Oh, don't worry about it," Molly said.

"Do you need help with anything?" Jack asked.

"I could use a little bit of Sarah's help, if that's all right." Ida Mae turned her bright eyes in Molly's direction, and she stood. She had no idea what Ida Mae could possibly need her help for—Jack was the homemaker in their partnership.

Molly set the table following Ida Mae's instructions, then arranged the rolls in a bread basket.

"I hope you don't mind a question, but something's been preying on my mind and I know I won't get any peace until I ask you about it." Ida Mae paused on her way to the table, holding a full gravy boat with both hands. "Do you mind?"

"It all depends." Molly placed the rolls on the table. "Does it have something to do with the case? There are things I can't tell you—"

Ida Mae shook her head, then set the gravy down by the potatoes. "It doesn't have anything to do with the case, dear. I know you can't tell me everything, even though I am dying of curiosity. It's about you and Jason. How long have you been having marital problems?"

Molly's breath caught in her throat. She thought they'd hidden it so well—how did Ida Mae know?

She continued before Molly could voice her question. "I'm an old woman, but my eyes are still sharp. You're not sleeping in the same bed—when you asked my advice on an outfit for church your first Sunday here, only half the bed was rumpled. The other half was perfectly tucked in."

"Bed making and I are not on the best of terms."

Ida Mae smiled. "And I noticed that the cushions on the couch were slightly askew all the way down the length, as if someone had stretched out there. If two people had been sitting there, only two of the cushions would have been a little off. And there was a corner of a blanket peeking out from beneath the couch, as though it had been shoved there in a hurry."

"You are a good detective," Molly admitted.

"Thank you. But your clues were rather obvious."

Molly sat on one of the stools that lined the counter. "We've been struggling for the last little bit, and a few days before getting this assignment, we decided to divorce."

"Oh, dear." Ida Mae sat on the kitchen chair closest to Molly's stool. "I'm so sorry. And I don't mean to be intrusive. It's just that you and Jason seem so perfect together. You have your careers in common, and you're so cute, and he's, well . . ." She leaned forward. "Don't tell Arlette I said this, but Jason's a hottie."

Molly snorted before her laugh formed itself properly. "Hottie?"

"Well, aren't I right?"

"You are. I just didn't think you'd use that word."

"If a word is accurate, I see no reason to waste time and brain cells in finding a different one." Ida Mae straightened the fork on the table near her elbow. "Can I give you some advice?"

"I'd love some. I've been so lost—I haven't known what to do."

"George is my second husband, and we've only been married for about a year."

"Really? I wouldn't have guessed."

"You might even call us newlyweds." Ida Mae's gaze became a little dreamy. "George swept me off my feet the moment I met him. Well, to be honest, I was already off my feet—I was in a wheelchair. And perhaps it wasn't the very first moment—I was somewhat distracted by his toupee, which has since been burned. But I digress. We had a lot of challenges to overcome. He is rather wealthy, and his children didn't want him leaving his huge house to come live here with me, but I knew I wasn't cut out for his more elegant lifestyle. He made that sacrifice for me. Oh, he still has money, but it's just not as obvious. He gave up a lot of prestige so we could live a simple life together."

"That's really romantic." And very selfless.

"The thing is, Sarah, I would have done the same for him. If he'd been unable to give up his home, I would have sold mine. I wanted to be where he was, just as he wanted to be where I was. We compromised because we wanted to be together."

"So you think Jason and I need to find some compromises in our situation," Molly said.

"Absolutely. Ask yourself what you want more—to be right, or to be married. I might have gotten that from Dr. Phil—it's hard to remember. Anyway, I don't know all your problems, and I don't want to know. It's really none of my business. But if there's one thing I do know, it's that relationships are precious. I understand that sometimes you really do need to let go, but other times, they're worth hanging on to with everything you've got."

Molly thought about Ida Mae's words all through dinner and after dessert. What was she willing to compromise to keep Jack? And was she more determined to be right than she was to stay married? Snuggling down to sleep in a bed much too large for just one person, she knew she had her answer—she was willing to do whatever it took. She just didn't have any idea what that might be.

NINETEEN

It had been a very busy week. A funeral for a murder victim, a Relief Society dinner, a nice evening spent at the bishop's house, and now a meet-and-greet with the Mafia. Molly chuckled a little as she thought about that. She'd wager that last night's dinner and tonight's would be worlds apart.

She dug around in the back of the closet and pulled out the box of clothes she'd tucked there when they moved in. She was glad she'd brought it—she doubted she'd be able to find any mobster's girlfriend clothes in Omni, and she didn't want to waste time shopping anyway.

She pulled back the cardboard flaps and began to dig through the layers until she found what she wanted—a navy-blue sequined mini dress with long sleeves and a plunging back. She found her four-inch stilettos, too, and her dangling earrings. She put them all on the bed while she started to change, and then was struck by an awful thought.

"Jack," she called through the door, "I don't know who I am."

"I think the Mormons would have some answers for you about that," he replied from the living room.

"That's not what I mean. What's my name? I mean, what's Joe Baker's girlfriend's name?"

Jack was silent for a moment. "I don't think we were ever told. Let me call Agent Blevins."

Molly brushed her hair and added a few more coats of makeup, then put on her jewelry. When she came out of the bedroom, Jack was just hanging up the phone.

"He asked Tony. Turns out Joe had a different girlfriend every month, so you could choose about any name you wanted."

Molly paused. She wasn't used to choosing her own name—they were usually chosen for her.

"Lolita," she said, striking a dramatic pose.

"No."

"Angelica."

"Don't think so."

"Francesca."

Jack pulled a face.

"Oh, come on. You said I could choose any name I wanted."

"I should have amended that to 'any name within reason.' Remember, you're the girlfriend. Like an accessory. You shouldn't be too memorable. We can use you best that way."

Molly sighed. "Like the secret weapon?"

"Exactly."

She didn't mind being the secret weapon. In fact, she rather enjoyed it most of the time, coming out of the shadows and doing her thing when no one was watching. But secret weapons never got cool names.

"All right, how about Mindy? That's a cute name, but not too outrageous, and not too far from my own."

"That will work."

Molly paused. She hadn't noticed when she first came out of the room that Jack was wearing a very sharp suit. "You look nice," she said.

"Thanks. So do you."

She did a little modeling turn to hide the flush creeping up her cheeks. Why was she blushing at a compliment from her husband? She felt about seventeen, getting picked up by her date for the prom.

"Oh, wait." She slid the wedding band off her finger and set it on the bookcase. "Can't wear that."

"You'll want this, though." Jack reached into his pocket and pulled out a diamond-and-ruby ring. "Joe Baker likes giving gifts to his ladies."

Molly nearly choked when she took the ring and studied the design. "Is this thing real?"

"Yes, but it's a loaner. Blevins wants it back."

"This belongs to Blevins?"

Jack smirked. "Not really his style. No, the agency footed the bill, and our hides will be forfeit if anything happens to it."

"I kind of like my hide. Can I leave the ring here and just pretend I wore it?"

"It's part of the cover, Molly."

She slid it onto her finger. Despite the heart attack she was having over the consequences if she lost the ring, she had to admit it looked mighty nice on her hand. She wiggled her fingers, and the stones sparkled. "I could get used to this."

"That's good, because any time you're out as Mindy, you'll be wearing it."

They climbed into the car and began the drive to Fabiano's party. Molly couldn't get comfortable in her seat and realized how much it was bothering her not to be armed. She was so used to having a gun at the small of her back and another on her ankle, that to be without her weapons made her feel like something was horribly wrong.

"I miss my guns." She tried to comfort herself that she had great legs and taking off the ankle holster let her show them to their best advantage.

"You know you couldn't wear them tonight. Why would Mindy need a gun?"

"I'm jealous. You still get yours."

"I am an assassin. Assassins get guns."

"Why can't I be your assassiny girlfriend?"

"Assassiny?"

"You know what I mean. Why can't I be an assassin too?"

"I wear the holster in this relationship."

Molly settled back in her seat, trying to focus on the job they were about to do. She couldn't let something like her total gunlessness distract her.

The hotel Fabiano had chosen for the cocktail party was one of the nicest Molly had ever seen, and for a moment, she wondered if they'd left Utah and gone through some kind of wormhole through time and space. Who would have thought these humble mountains were hiding a place like this? Marble columns, carpet so thick she almost fell over when she tried to walk on it in her high heels, fine artwork on the walls—this wasn't your mama's Motel 8.

Jack and Molly were greeted by Sean as they entered the large room off the lobby. "So glad you could make it," he said. "Please, come meet Mr. Fabiano. He's been asking about you."

Molly glanced at the large clock that hung over the fireplace in the corner. "I'm sorry if we're late."

"Oh, no, you're right on time. Mr. Fabiano has just been looking forward to this meeting, that's all."

Jack and Molly followed Sean through the crowd of people to the back corner of the room, where Fabiano sat on a red velvet couch. The picture Molly had seen in Agent Blevins' office had either been taken a good decade earlier, or it had been photoshopped. In that picture, the man had jowls, but in real life, they were so pronounced he looked like a basset hound. Which wasn't necessarily a bad thing—Molly liked basset hounds—but she did wonder if they flapped when he talked.

"Mr. Fabiano, this is Joe Baker." Sean made the introduction, then stepped aside. Jack nodded once, but didn't say anything.

"And who is this lovely young lady?" Fabiano asked, his jowls not flapping, to Molly's relief.

"I'm Mindy," she said. "This is a lovely party, Mr. Fabiano."

He smiled, and Molly caught a glimpse of the charm that had radiated from his photograph. She realized what was missing—he looked happy in the picture, and tonight, he seemed as though a great many things were bothering him. "Please, enjoy yourselves. Eat, drink—and if you want something but don't see it, just ask the wait staff. My treat."

"Thank you. That's really nice of you."

Fabiano turned his attention to Jack. "Your reputation precedes you, as they say."

"As does yours."

Fabiano chuckled. "I'm sure it will come as no surprise that I've looked forward to this meeting with, shall we say, a certain amount of anticipation." He stood and began walking toward the buffet, still talking. Jack and Molly fell into step behind him. "I'm not as young as I once was. I rely on others to do things I used to do myself. You don't know yet what it means to get old, but someday you will, and then you'll understand."

He came to a stop and motioned expansively with his arm. "Please, make yourselves a plate of food, and then let's talk."

Molly filled her plate, impressed with the selection—caviar and paté, brioche and crudités—then followed Jack to the private alcove where Fabiano now sat, a flute of champagne at his elbow.

"Eat, eat," Fabiano encouraged. "I can't talk business on an empty stomach, and I don't expect anyone else to either."

The conversation ceased as Jack and Molly ate. She had never tasted such amazing caviar, and told Fabiano as much.

He laughed. "Joe, you really need to get this young lady out more. A girl such as this should have all the finer things in life."

"I agree," Molly said. She glanced over at Jack, who quirked an eyebrow at her.

When they'd had their fill, a waiter appeared and took their plates, and Fabiano settled more comfortably into his chair.

"I've heard an interesting rumor," he said, stroking the fabric on the armrest. "It appears that a dead body was found in your floral shop."

"True," Jack replied.

"Was he one of yours?"

Jack threw back his head and laughed. "No. Mine aren't so . . . tactlessly displayed. It was a coincidence, nothing more."

Fabiano smiled. "I thought as much. A man of your reputation would never have been so careless. Now, I trust that Mindy won't be too bored if we talk business." He looked at her. "Would you rather go meet the other ladies? I believe they're over by the chocolate fountain."

Molly paused. She wanted to stay and hear everything. Scratch that—she was *dying* to stay. But Fabiano's suggestion had carried a deeper implication, and she knew she was being dismissed. "I hope you'll excuse me, but a girl's got to have chocolate."

Fabiano rose when she stood. "Enjoy."

She wiggled her fingers in a brief wave, then stepped back out to the main party area. The chocolate fountain wasn't hard to find, and she wondered why she hadn't spotted it before. Things like that usually called to her like a siren's song. Eight or ten women were clustered in groups nearby, many holding small dishes of melted chocolate and nibbling daintily at the foods they'd chosen to dip. Molly walked over and checked out the assortment, and then decided this was as close to heaven as she would ever get. She didn't know what the Mormons thought about heaven—whether they pictured angels on fluffy clouds playing harps or what—but if she ever found a religion that promised a chocolate fountain as an eternal reward, she'd sign on the dotted line.

"Hello. We haven't met."

Molly looked up and saw a stunningly beautiful woman standing beside her. She was probably in her early fifties, but her face was smooth and her hair was a gorgeous shade of rich brown. "Hi. I'm Mindy."

"And I'm Cassandra Fabiano. I believe my husband is having a 'secret' meeting with your boyfriend." She smiled and winked. "These men and their business deals. They tuck themselves away for hours on end to discuss things we'd have figured out in thirty seconds. Are you enjoying yourself?"

"Very much. I was just trying to decide between the strawberries and the raspberries."

Cassandra waved a well-manicured hand. "Try them all. That's the only way you'll really be sure."

Molly certainly didn't have to be told twice. She helped herself to one of everything that looked good, knowing full well she'd never be able to eat it all, and then nodded as Cassandra introduced her to the other ladies.

It was odd, walking around at a mobster's party, meeting all his mobster friends and eating all his mobster food, as though this were a gathering of ordinary people. What was perhaps the most odd was that everyone was pretending they really *were* ordinary. They spoke of "business" and "meetings" as though they were accountants or bankers, and Molly found it amusing and disconcerting at the same time.

"Do you enjoy going to the spa?" one of the ladies asked, turning to focus on Molly.

"Who doesn't?"

"Exactly." The woman laughed, and Molly tried to remember her name. Angela, that was it. Molly had been listening to Cassandra's introductions, but her mind kept wandering to the conversation between Jack and Fabiano. She knew Jack would tell her everything later, but she liked getting her information firsthand.

"You should come with us," another woman said. Her name was Patrice. Molly snapped her attention back into place—she'd better get to know these women. The information they might let slip could be very helpful to the case.

"I would love that," she said. "When are you going?"

"Tomorrow morning. Do you know where Aspen Ridge Lodge is?"

"I'm sorry, I don't. We've only lived here a couple of weeks."

"It's all right—I'll send a car for you," Cassandra said. "Be ready at nine."

"That would be wonderful. Thank you."

Jack walked up, and all the women turned toward him like he was some kind of magnet forcing their heads to swivel his direction. "Is this a ladies' only corner?" he asked.

"Of course not," Angela said. "Please join us. And have some chocolate."

Jack picked up a bowl and began to help himself, and Angela whispered to Molly, "Is that yours? He's possibly the best-looking man I've ever seen."

"Yeah, I know," she said, allowing herself to sound a little smug. She remembered the first time she saw Jack. He had taken her breath away, but she'd had to get it back right quick because they were being pursued and she had to have enough oxygen to run. She knew the effect he was having on these women and she really shouldn't care, but she did. A lot.

"Let me tell you about the spa." Patrice tucked her arm though Molly's. "They have the most amazing mud baths . . ."

"So?" Molly said as soon as she and Jack retrieved their car from the valet and pulled out of the hotel parking lot. She'd kept a smile plastered on her face the entire evening, and she was anxious for a report. It was hard, pretending to be patient.

Jack exhaled slowly. "I'm not even sure where to start."

"Start with all the good stuff and work backwards."

He nodded, even though she knew he wouldn't do it that way. He was very linear—he had to start at the beginning and work his way to the end. It drove her nuts sometimes, but it did make things more logical.

"Fabiano looks upon this new relationship with Scarlotti as the answer to his problems. Scarlotti's twenty years younger, he's got his finger on the pulse of the underground world, and Fabiano feels that this merger will save his business. He's not a healthy man, Molly. He's got congestive heart failure, and he's worried everything will fall apart when he goes. He's lost some of his most trusted men, he has no children, and he doesn't know who could take over for him."

"Wow. And he's going to be this open with Scarlotti? Doesn't that make him vulnerable? What if Scarlotti doesn't want a fair deal?"

"I wondered about that too," Jack said, "but Fabiano went on to tell me that he's had his lawyers go over everything, and he showed me some paperwork outlining the potential agreement. Fabiano may be getting older and he may be sick, but he's certainly no fool. He's got this thing figured out to the last penny. He'll be fine."

"So are you supposed to take the paperwork to Scarlotti?"

"In a bit. Fabiano wanted to solidify something else first—he didn't say what. But he'll tell me when he's ready." Jack paused to negotiate a tricky curve in the road. "How was your night?"

"It was okay—lots of chocolate, and gossip about people I don't know. And I've been invited to go to the spa tomorrow."

"That's a great idea. Get yourself in good with the ladies of the organization."

"Yeah, I thought that would be helpful. Not sure what to do about the shop, though."

"Ask Tansy to cover it."

"You're right, I should." Molly looked out the window, just able to make out the silhouettes of trees in the moonlight. She certainly wasn't going to pass on letting someone else run the shop for a day—that would just be crazy.

"Doesn't it smell amazing?" Jack asked.

"What?"

Jack inhaled deeply. "Can't you smell that?" When Molly shook her head, he used the buttons on his console to roll down her window. She smelled it then—an earthy, woodsy, pine-laced smell that reminded her of one Thanksgiving spent with her folks in Virginia right after she finished training at Quantico. "Isn't it fantastic?" Jack said.

"Yeah." She closed her eyes, a rare wave of homesickness washing over her. Being an undercover agent was everything she'd ever dreamed it would be—it brought her excitement, adventure, the chance to play with guns as often as she wanted—but she disliked having to be apart from her family while on cases, unable to contact them at all. They were supportive and they understood, but she didn't like having to push them out of her thoughts so often to keep from missing them.

Molly was relieved to take off her party dress and climb into some fuzzy pajamas. She usually liked being the center of attention, but tonight, she wanted to be invisible, and she couldn't figure out why.

TWENTY

The alarm clock went off way earlier than Molly thought was compassionate. She was tempted to shoot it, but remembered she was going to the spa with the ladies of the mob this morning. Eyes suddenly wide open, she bounced out of bed and was in the shower before she realized she hadn't thought about coffee. Well, except she'd just thought about it when she realized she hadn't thought about it, but the point was that she was up, bathing, and somewhat functional without relying on a substance to get her going. Very interesting indeed.

Promptly at nine, a black limo pulled up in front of the house. As Molly hurried down the sidewalk, a uniformed driver opened the passenger door. Molly climbed in the car, smiling as her body sank into the rich leather seat. A snack bar in the corner featured a variety of breakfast foods. She didn't think she'd be able to eat anything after the sumptuous spread the night before, but she did help herself to a bagel, and some fruit, and a small glass of orange juice. Oh, and then there was the tiny cheese Danish . . .

When the limo pulled up at the spa, Molly stepped out into paradise. The place had a definite Shinto feel, from the wooden arches to the koi pond in the circular driveway, to the quiet staff who moved around on bare feet, hardly speaking. Angela met her just inside the doors and guided her into the first room, where she was given a thick robe and slippers to wear. She tucked her own things into a locker and tightened the sash around her waist. Once again, she missed her gun, but decided it probably wouldn't have worked to wear it to a spa anyway—she might get muck from the mud bath in the barrel, and that wouldn't be good.

Molly had never tried to conduct an investigation while having a massage, or a pedicure, or a manicure. She was so relaxed that it was difficult to concentrate on anything, and she fought not to drift off to sleep.

The ladies were a bit of a disappointment. Oh, they were friendly, and they welcomed Molly right in and included her in all their conversations, but there wasn't any useful gossip. She didn't care that Trixie O'Neil had a facelift or that Margo James was having an affair—she wanted them to talk about the organization or to mention Fabiano's secret hideout, but nothing. It was like the mob world didn't even exist to them. And then she realized maybe it didn't. These women might think of their husbands' careers like a plumber's wife might think of his job, or a carpenter's wife might think of his—it pays the bills, and she doesn't really get involved in all the details.

"Mindy, tell us something about Joe," Patrice said languidly as they ate their lunch on the spa patio. "I hear someone was killed in your shop."

"Patrice, hush," Angela reprimanded.

"No, it's all right. I imagine you're curious." Molly glanced around the table. These ladies might not be involved with the mob per se, but they knew what was what. "He wasn't one of Joe's. It was all a bizarre coincidence."

"That's what my husband said." Cassandra motioned to the waiter. "Let's all have another lemonade. We don't need to make Mindy feel uncomfortable on her first day with us."

"That's right. We can grill you another time," Angela said with a laugh.

"I just figured, what with him being Joe Baker and all . . ." Patrice seemed determined to pursue this line of questioning.

"He's not responsible for every dead body in the world." Angela stirred her drink with her straw.

"I didn't mean to imply anything." Patrice laid her hand on Molly's arm, her newly manicured nails standing out blood red against the white sleeve of Molly's robe. "Please, let's be friends."

"Of course." Molly returned the woman's smile but wondered, was Patrice asking out of curiosity? Because she had almost sounded vindictive, and Molly wasn't sure why.

Rather than calling the limo to take Molly home, Cassandra offered her a ride in a sleek black sports car that made Molly drool. She wondered if mob assassins made enough for a car like this. She wouldn't mind having one—as part of her cover, of course.

"Don't worry about Patrice," Cassandra said as they got underway. "Her husband has done some work for our family in the past and she might be feeling a little bit replaced. But we all know that Joe's on loan and he belongs to Scarlotti. I think Patrice will get over it."

So, Patrice's husband was Fabiano's regular hit man. That was good to know. "Thanks," Molly said. "I did wonder if I'd done something to offend her."

"She gets offended pretty easily. You should have seen her this Easter when we were organizing the egg hunt for the hospital. She could have laid some of those eggs herself, she was so riled up about something. Now I don't even remember what, but you just have to take her with a grain of salt. She'll come around."

"Does that mean I can come with you again some time?" The hope Molly infused into her voice wasn't entirely made up—if these women took her in, she'd be a lot more useful to the investigation than just a flower maker.

"Of course." Cassandra took her eyes off the road long enough to flick a warm glance at Molly. "Nick liked Joe a lot. We stayed up a long time last night talking about him."

"Nick? Oh, Mr. Fabiano? I didn't know his first name. I'm glad he likes Joe. It makes things easier."

"Yes, it certainly does." Cassandra brought her car to a stop in front of Molly's house. "I'll give you a call next week and we'll do lunch, all right? I get together with the other wives on Wednesdays, so see if you can keep your afternoons free."

"I'd really like that." Molly waved goodbye and headed inside, feeling that she was finally making a contribution to the team.

Everyone gathered in the dining room at Jack and Molly's house. She was eager to see what the ladies had learned. Jack hadn't found any evidence that John Ferguson was in contact with any of his old drug-using friends from high school, and once again, the investigation was going nowhere.

Ida Mae whipped out a notebook and placed it on the table. It was purple, which didn't surprise Molly at all. It seemed everything Ida Mae owned was purple.

"Tansy covered all the shops on the west side of the street, and Arlette took all the shops on the east," Ida Mae reported. "Neither of them got any new information. The street was quiet all morning long until the emergency vehicles arrived."

"I did find out Misty Clements is expecting twins," Tansy put in. "But I don't suppose that's relevant."

"Not so much, although it is interesting," Jack said. "Ida Mae, what did you find out?"

"I spoke to the shopkeepers through the block—you know, the ones who share alleys with the stores on Main Street? Most of them were working toward the front of their stores, or hadn't even made it in to work yet when the murder took place. You guys got an awfully early start that day."

"I know," Molly said. "And I'm still missing a couple hours of sleep because of it."

Ida Mae leaned forward. "I do have one small piece of information." Her eyes held a twinkle, like she knew what Molly was getting for Christmas. "Marty Booth, who owns Booth's Bakery, was out back putting some trash in his Dumpster when he saw someone leaving your shop through the back door. Just a moment or two later, he saw you and Jack pull up. You missed the perpetrator by a whisker."

Molly leaned forward too. "And did Marty get a good look?"

"No. The way your building is situated, it casts a shadow. All Marty could tell was that he was tall and dressed in black or navy blue."

Molly spun Jack's laptop around, which was open to the police report. There—the police had spoken to Marty, but since he couldn't see the person's face, there was little to go on. No wonder the police investigation had come to a halt.

"We just don't know enough," Molly said at last.

"If I might make a suggestion." Arlette looked up from knitting a magenta sock. She'd been quiet during this little meeting, which was highly suspicious in and of itself. "You're looking for new information without stopping to consider what you *do* know."

"That's a very good point, Arlette." Ida Mae turned to a clean sheet in her notebook. "What do we know?"

"We know that whoever killed John Ferguson either put the drugs in the wall, or knew the drugs were in the wall. We have no other motive at this time," Molly said.

"But do we really, *really* know that? What if John had been cheating on Danyelle, and she came to the shop all angry and stuff?" Tansy shook her head. "I'm not saying that's the case—just that sometimes things happen that aren't related."

Molly sighed. She didn't want to allow room for this theory, but she had to look at every possibility. "True, not every murder is committed for the most obvious reasons. However, I think if the murder wasn't drug related, it's too much of a coincidence that John was killed in front of a wall containing drugs and then the loose brick went missing. That would be like the plot of a really corny detective novel where the author was trying too hard to throw in some red herrings."

Ida Mae nodded. "Yes, it's far too much of a coincidence. I think we need to concentrate on the drug angle."

"We know that whoever killed John Ferguson knew he was in the shop," Tansy said.

"But did he know John would be there, or did he go to the shop to retrieve the drugs and just happen on John in the middle of the repairs?" Arlette asked.

Ida Mae shook her head. "That's another pretty outrageous coincidence. Those drugs were in the wall for . . . how long? He could have come back at any time, and yet he stumbled on the exact minute when John was there? I think he knew."

"That means he planned to kill John, and timed his visit accordingly." Molly stood and went into the kitchen to grab the bag of Doritos from the cupboard. "Sorry, I need brain food." She plunked the chips down on the table and popped one into her mouth. "Help yourself. But don't take too many because then there won't be enough left for me."

Her brain swirled while she chewed. "If our perpetrator came to the shop on purpose while John was there, he must have had it in for him. For some reason, he needed John out of the way."

"That would indicate someone from John's drug-related past, wouldn't it?" Arlette asked.

"It would. We haven't found anything suspicious in his recent activity, though. No contact with questionable friends—nothing."

"But you're forgetting something," Jack inserted. "John came in as a replacement for Roger. Was John the real target, or was it Roger?"

Molly grabbed more chips.

"But what if . . . what if he came to the shop when John was there because that's the only time he could get into the shop without you knowing?" Ida Mae's eyes glittered again. "What if he needed a way to circumvent the security system, and he knew that because John was there, you'd have things dialed down a notch for him?"

"So John was just in the way instead of being an intended victim," Molly finished.

"But if the perp didn't have a way inside the shop, how did he get the drugs in the wall in the first place?" Arlette wanted to know.

Ida Mae sighed. "I keep telling you, real law enforcement officers don't use the word 'perp.' That's only on television."

"Okay—bad guy. Does that work?"

"Much better."

Arlette turned back to Molly. "If the bad guy didn't have access to the shop, how did the drugs get in the wall?"

Molly grinned. "Easy. Esther didn't have a security system, and we changed the locks. We're looking for someone who used to have a key to the shop or could break into it easily, but doesn't have a key or the security codes now."

"You aren't suggesting . . ." Tansy's face was a mask of horror.

"What?"

"That Esther's behind all this, are you?"

"No, of course not." Although Molly did have to think about it for a second. If three little old ladies could solve crimes, one little old lady could perpetrate them, couldn't she? Molly shook her head. She had a good imagination, but she just couldn't stretch it that far.

"You three have been very helpful," she said. "Have a Dorito. You've earned it."

"If it's not Esther . . ." Tansy looked thoughtful while she chewed, which was a funny combination.

"I hate to say it, but I think I've narrowed down our list of suspects to just one," Molly said.

"The only person who comes to my mind is Ryan," Jack said. "He was one of Esther's most trusted employees, and he mentioned once that he had a key to the shop so he could open for her when her arthritis was flaring up. Plus, he was there when I called Roger to fix the wall, so he knew when to come back."

Molly sighed. "That's who I fingered too, but I don't feel entirely good about it. He's a decent kid. I don't see him murdering anyone."

"I like him too, but that doesn't mean he's not guilty," Jack said. "We've collared plenty of guys we never would have pegged based on their personalities alone."

"I know, I know. But he's just a kid." They'd arrested kids before. They'd arrested really innocent-looking, puppy-dog-eyed kids who burst into tears and insisted they were innocent until the evidence came back to bite them and they were proven guilty of some really heinous crimes. Molly couldn't let Ryan's age get in the way of her investigation. "All right, I guess it's time to narrow our focus," she said. "What have we got on Ryan?"

"I ran that background check on him before we hired him—I don't think another check would turn up anything new," Jack replied.

"Then we need to do some other digging—talking to his friends, his family."

"I just don't know," Ida Mae said. "I understand you can't rule anyone out on reputation alone, but I've known Ryan since before he was born—well, you know what I mean. His parents moved to Omni right after they were married. I've never seen him do anything remotely illegal—"

"I wouldn't be too hasty," Arlette interrupted. "You don't know everything, Ida Mae."

"I might not know everything, but I do know quite a bit. Former Relief Society president, current bishop's wife—wait. What do you know that you're not telling me?"

Arlette looked more than a little bit smug that she had information Ida Mae didn't, and Molly was willing to bet this didn't happen all that often. "Ryan's girlfriend is in rehab right now."

"Ryan has a girlfriend?" Tansy asked.

"She's in rehab?" Ida Mae raised an eyebrow. "Why didn't I know that?"

"Because they're keeping it under wraps. Her parents didn't want anyone to know."

"But I'm *supposed* to know everything about everyone."

"It's impossible to know everything," Molly reasoned. "And I'm sure her parents have a very good excuse for not telling you."

"Most likely, they're worried about her father's career," Tansy said complacently. "I would be too."

"What is her father's career?" Molly asked. "What's the girl's name?"

"Heidi Millhouse. Her father is the mayor of Omni."

"I see." Politicians had problems just like everyone else, but it was obviously more crucial for them to keep their problems hidden. If Molly remembered correctly from the dossier she read on the town of Omni as they drove here, the mayor had run on an anti-drug campaign. And he was up for reelection in about two weeks. "This is all starting to look a little shady."

Jack tapped rapidly on his laptop for a moment. "According to the information Blevins just sent over, Heidi has been a resident of the Hidden Vista Rehabilitation Village for the last thirty days and is a model patient."

"So, if the mayor didn't want anyone to know about his daughter's drug problem, and he learned that her boyfriend worked at a floral shop that was being used as a drop-off point for drugs, in his own town . . ." Molly paused. "How desperate do you think he'd be?"

"Are you saying that he would have hired Ryan to take care of it, or that he would have hired someone else to take care of Ryan?" Arlette asked.

"I don't know, actually," Molly said. "I think we should look at both scenarios."

"Don't forget that you gave Ryan an advance on his paycheck the other day," Jack put in.

"That's right—and then I heard him talking to someone on the phone, assuring them that he got the money."

Jack nodded slowly. "All right, ladies, we've got our work cut out for us. We're focusing in on Ryan. We're going to find out where he's been, what he's been up to. Ida Mae, can you talk to his mother?"

"Certainly."

"We need to find out how he spent the money he got from Sarah, how well he knows his girlfriend's father, and what he was doing the morning of the murder. We also need to look into Mayor Millhouse. Sarah and I will take care of that."

"What if I talked to Heidi's mother?" Tansy asked. "We are good friends, and I might be able to learn some things."

"That would be excellent." Jack had a new spark in his eye, and Molly imagined she did too. After two and a half weeks of absolutely nothing, they were finally getting somewhere.

"Let's meet up tomorrow night and discuss what we've learned," she suggested.

"I'm sorry, dear—can we make that Monday afternoon? It's Sunday tomorrow, and we try not to solve crimes on the Sabbath," Ida Mae said.

"Oh. Okay," Molly replied.

"Unless it's an emergency," Tansy added. "We wouldn't refuse to solve it if someone was bleeding to death, for instance."

"Good to know. Okay, let's make it Monday at four at the shop, all right?" Jack said. He rose when the ladies stood and escorted them to the door, calling out "good night" just before they drove away.

"I'm not sure how I like Ryan for the bad guy," Molly said. She was running out of Doritos and would need more before the night was over—this warranted a trip to the grocery store.

"He's the most likely suspect we've got," Jack said. "I'm not saying I like it any better than you do, but we have to be realistic here, Molly. We're running out of options, so we have to concentrate on the ones we have. And if he's innocent, we're helping to prove that."

She nodded. "I know. Let's get this thing solved so we can get back to bringing down the mob, shall we?"

TWENTY-ONE

Molly had a tingle in her chest, the one that told her they were on the right track and they'd soon have this case solved. She wanted to bring closure to the Fergusons, and she wanted to get one more murderer off the street. Even if he was just a teenage boy.

Jack had spent an hour chatting with Braden via the Internet, and they'd looked into all the available files on Mayor Millhouse. Some had required special FBI access, so Blevins stepped in to wield the proper authority. By the time Ida Mae, Arlette, and Tansy showed up at the floral shop Monday afternoon, Molly felt there was something concrete to discuss. She'd given Ryan the day off so they wouldn't be interrupted, but promised him more hours later in the week so he could honor his agreement to pay back that hundred dollars. Of course, if they ended up arresting him, that wouldn't work so well.

Molly flipped the Open sign to Closed, and everyone gathered in the wedding consultation area. It was an odd place to discuss a murder, surrounded as they were by pictures of smiling brides and adorable flower girls, but it was the only place in the shop with enough chairs.

"We have a lot to tell you," Ida Mae said.

"And we have a lot to tell you," Jack replied.

Tansy looked conflicted. "But who should go first?"

"Let me start with what is perhaps the most important development," Jack said. "And then maybe we can take turns."

Tansy seemed pleased with that decision.

"Heidi Millhouse somehow gained access to drugs while in the rehab center and overdosed the other night."

"Oh, no! Is she all right?" Ida Mae asked.

"She'll be fine, but the center is conducting a private investigation into how she got the drugs. They had a visiting day last week, and Heidi's parents, sister, uncle, and boyfriend all showed up."

"Ryan visited Heidi at the rehab center after hitting you up for an advance, and then Heidi overdosed? Why am I feeling very suspicious right now?" Arlette asked.

"That is big news." Ida Mae leaned back in her chair. "Anything we offer is going to seem pretty insignificant after that."

"Nothing's insignificant," Molly said, and Jack nodded.

"Well, we found out Ryan had visited Heidi in rehab. His mother told us that," Ida Mae began. "But she didn't tell us about the overdose."

"She was probably cooperating with the center's investigation and keeping it quiet," Jack said.

"We also found out Ryan has been really involved with Heidi's drug problem," Ida Mae continued. "He went with her to talk to her school counselor when she admitted her addiction, and he apparently knew her drug dealer. Mrs. Millhouse said he seemed to know a lot about her daughter's condition."

"Mrs. Millhouse was really nice and talked to us for an hour about it," Tansy said. "She and I have known each other for a long time, and she let us right in. I think she wants to help Heidi in any way she can."

"Except she didn't tell us about the overdose," Arlette added.

"Is it possible she didn't know about it?" Ida Mae asked.

"It's extremely unlikely," Jack said. "Heidi's a minor, so the center would be obligated to report any serious incidents to her parents. Mrs. Millhouse was just cooperating with the investigation, I'm sure."

Everyone shared the information they'd picked up. Braden called in and said he hadn't found anything useful to their investigation in the mayor's files, although Agent Blevins had flagged a few things to check out later. Jack had discovered that Ryan never deposited his paychecks—he only cashed them, even though he had a checking account. "The total in that account is twenty-three dollars and eleven cents," Jack reported. "Apparently, he likes using cash better than debit cards."

"So do I," Tansy said. "It's so much easier to see how much money I have."

"And cash is also harder to trace," Jack pointed out.

"I learned from Ryan's mother that he's been gone a lot lately," Ida Mae said. "Of course, she knows about his shift here, but beyond that, she doesn't know where he is much of the time."

"That actually sounds pretty typical of a boy his age," Molly said. "Out of high school, not yet in college, hasn't decided what to do with his life. That doesn't necessarily mean he's up to something illegal."

"But when added to these other details, it does become pertinent," Jack said.

Ida Mae reached into her large shoulder bag and pulled out a Tupperware container filled with cookies. "Doritos might be your brain food, Sarah, but cookies are mine." She passed them around and everyone fell to munching.

"So, what else do we know?" Tansy asked after a minute or two.

"We know that Ryan was one hundred dollars richer than usual, he went to see Heidi, and she overdosed," Molly replied. "We need to question him—find out if he did a little shopping on his way to the rehab center."

"Agreed," Jack said. "But with her history of drug use, could she really have overdosed on only a hundred dollars' worth of drugs?"

Molly crunched another chip. "You're right—it would probably take more than that. Unless she mixed it with something else. Do we know what drug she took?"

Jack checked his laptop. "Looks like heroin and Xanax."

Molly nodded. "Okay, you can get that for a hundred dollars, but that combination is pretty much an instant overdose. If Ryan brought those into the clinic for her, he'd know what he was doing. Was he trying to help her commit suicide, and they failed? What was their intention?"

"Maybe Heidi was trying to make a break from rehab and thought overdosing would give her some opportunities to give her caretakers the slip," Jack said. "She might have planned to take off from the hospital."

"Whatever her intentions, it certainly backfired." Ida Mae shook her head. "To go through all that trouble and end up right back in rehab anyway—it's a waste of planning and effort. Well, we can only conjecture at this point. What else do we know?"

"We assume the mayor was unaware that the floral shop was involved in drug sales," Jack said.

"You didn't tell us that before." Tansy sounded hurt.

"Sorry. We were covering a lot of things at once." Jack handed Tansy another cookie from the bowl on the table, and all seemed to be forgiven.

"Do you three have anything else to share?" Molly asked.

"Nothing beyond what we've already talked about. Several people mentioned seeing Ryan and Heidi together a lot, but none of them mentioned anything that stood out as being unusual," Ida Mae said.

"Was Ryan planning to serve a mission for your church?" Jack asked.

"I'm not sure," Ida Mae replied. "He's been talking to George recently, but I don't know what about. George isn't allowed to share confidential information with me."

"Why do you ask?" Arlette inquired.

"If he had been planning to serve at some point, it would seem that those plans have changed. He's of age now, and yet has nothing in the bank. He did have money two years ago—a fairly healthy sum, in fact—but it's been siphoned away bit by bit since then," Jack said.

"Are you saying that Ryan has been financing Heidi's drug habit over a long period of time?" Ida Mae asked.

"I'm saying it's a possibility. Having a healthy bank balance is unusual for a teenager unless he's saving up for something he really wants, like a car or college—or in this case, possibly a mission. But something happened about two years ago to make him decide to stop saving."

"He and Heidi have been together about two years," Tansy said.

"I think it's time to start asking the young man some questions," Jack said.

Molly dialed. "Ryan, I changed my mind. Can you come in today after all?"

Ryan headed straight for the broom when he reached the shop, as usual. Molly stopped him. "We need to talk."

He sat on the stool, nervousness written all over his face. "Is this about the money? Because I promise, I'll work it off in no time."

"It is about the money, but not the way you think." Molly took a deep breath before plunging into the lie. "Ryan, Mrs. Millhouse was in here earlier. She told me something I think you should know."

"Mrs. Millhouse? What's the matter? Is it Heidi?"

Molly held up a hand. "Just calm down, Ryan. Everything will be all right. Heidi's getting the best possible care."

Ryan jumped up and the stool crashed to the floor. "What are you talking about? What's wrong with her?"

"She got hold of some drugs the other day and overdosed."

"No!" Ryan slammed his hand on the counter, making the ceramic mug full of knives rattle. "This wasn't supposed to happen!"

"What was supposed to happen, Ryan?" Molly asked gently.

His eyes were filled with tears when he turned to face her. "The money I got from you was to pay off Heidi's dealer. He'd given her some stuff on credit, you know, because he wanted to keep her business. Right before she went into rehab, he threatened her, telling her that she'd better get the money or he'd go after her sister. She was able to scrape some together, but still needed a hundred dollars. Well, this new patient comes into rehab the other day, and it turns out he was there to give Heidi a message. He told her that she had three days to come up with the cash or her sister's pretty face wouldn't be so pretty anymore. She managed to call me, and that's when I asked you for the advance. I went and met with the guy and paid him off."

"You're telling me that money from my cash register went to a drug dealer?"

"I'm sorry, I really am. But I couldn't just let them go after her sister, could I? She's only twelve."

"You're right. You had to step in somehow, but I'm not sure that was the best way to go about it. You should have asked for help, Ryan."

"Well, I couldn't talk to the police! They're no good at all."

Molly pressed her lips together. Probably wouldn't be the best idea to put the kid on the floor and teach him some respect for law enforcement.

"Ryan, how did Heidi get the drugs in the center? Did you bring them to her?"

"Me? No!" His eyes took on a panicked look. "I've been trying to help her get off them for two years. I've taken her to the clinic when she got sick, I've tried to get her dealer to leave her alone—it's because of me that she's in rehab right now. Why on earth would I bring drugs to her in rehab?"

"Do you know who did?"

Ryan shook his head. "I don't. Unless it was the guy who delivered the message. But how'd he get them in there? Don't they search everyone who comes in that place?"

"You promise me it wasn't you?"

Ryan met Molly's gaze square on. "I promise you, I did not bring Heidi drugs in rehab."

She looked back at him for a long moment. "Very well. But listen to me—if you hear anything about who might have done it, you come tell me, all right? I have friends who can help. You can't keep trying to fight this on your own—there are people who are trained in drug abuse and recovery. Okay?"

"Thanks, Sarah. I will. I'll tell you anything I find out."

"And no more talking to drug dealers. That was, if you'll forgive my saying so, completely stupid."

"I promise."

Molly told Ryan he could leave again because she was getting ready to close up. "But be here on time tomorrow."

"I will."

The bell on the door rang as he left, and Molly walked back into the consultation area, her head reeling. "Quite the day of revelations," she said.

"Yeah." Jack seemed preoccupied with his laptop.

"What are you doing?"

"Oh, just double-checking the files at the rehab center. They aren't happy about it, but they gave Blevins access because of the overdose. Turns out, a new guy was brought in the other day, only he's not so new—this is his third time through the program. I think he might be the one who delivered the message to Heidi."

"So do you believe Ryan, then?" Molly asked.

"I'm not completely sure what I believe. All I know is that every shred of evidence we have points to him, and yet it's not satisfactory. He's just a kid."

"Oh, come on. The last time I said he was just a kid, you got all logical on me."

"Yeah, I know. And I was probably being unfair." Jack closed his laptop and smiled, a long, slow smile that covered his whole face and made his dimples show. "I need to check in with HQ, and after that, let me take you out to dinner. And then let's go grocery shopping and get some more real food."

"You do have a way of making a girl's heart go pitter-pat." Molly grabbed her purse and they closed up, double-checking the security system before they climbed into the car and drove toward Omni's nearest family restaurant, Pearsons' Place.

They were greeted at the door by Betty Pearson herself, a pretty blonde woman who introduced herself and then led them to a nice table in the corner. She explained the daily special, then left them alone while they decided what to get. Molly didn't care what she ate—she was just starving.

While they waited for their food, she watched Jack across the table. The flecks in his eyes danced in the reflection from the battery-operated candle in the center of the table. She surmised that in a family restaurant, you couldn't very well have an open flame—little Johnny might stick his hand right in it. Whatever the reason for the artificial nod toward romance, she had to admit she liked the way the soft glow lit her husband's face.

"We're so close, Molly," he said. "I can feel it."

"Me too. What did Braden say when you called him?"

"He's checking out the drug dealer and also this guy in rehab. He thinks we're on to something too—his sixth sense is going off."

"Do you think the dealer is responsible for John Ferguson's death?"

Jack shrugged. "I don't know if he's directly responsible, but he probably knows who did it. Let's keep our fingers crossed that he does, and that we're able to track him down soon."

The meal came, it was delicious, and Betty stopped by to make sure they'd enjoyed their time in her restaurant. "I'd like to talk to you about doing our holiday decorations this year," she said to Molly. "I want everything to look really festive."

"I'd enjoy that. Why don't you come in next week, and we can talk about it?"

Betty picked a day and time, and Molly plugged it into her phone, along with a note to bring Tansy in on the consultation.

As Jack and Molly drove home, she couldn't ignore the feeling that was bubbling up inside her. Jack looked so good tonight, and he'd been wonderful during dinner. He'd even been especially kind and thoughtful while they were at the grocery store, choosing her favorite brands instead of his own, buying ingredients to make things he knew she'd like. It was like being newlyweds again, only with the knowledge that they would never have that back as long as they lived, and she couldn't bear it.

TWENTY-TWO

The ache in Molly's chest had grown too great for her to ignore. A glance at the clock told her it was after three. She'd pulled her sheets off the bed with all her tossing and turning. She had to talk to Jack—she had to get this out in the open. She tiptoed into the living room. Part of her hoped he was asleep—then she could justify putting this off until the next day. But she knew she'd get no peace until she did something proactive.

"Jack?" she said softly. His even breathing made her think he was out, but then he responded.

"Yeah?"

She sat on the overstuffed chair near the couch and pulled her feet up beneath her. The floor was cold, and she took a moment to tuck her long pajama legs around her toes to warm herself up. Jack rolled over and looked at her. She couldn't see the expression on his face, but she could tell he was fully awake, listening.

"Why do you want to divorce me?" There—she'd said it. But she didn't like *how* she'd said it, like a scared little girl seeking comfort and validation.

Jack was absolutely still. Then his voice came from the darkness. "I didn't ask for a divorce, Molly—you did."

Her heart stopped beating. What? She frantically thought back to their argument, the one that had started this whole thing. He'd said something—she couldn't remember what, just that it was really, really painful. She'd reacted from a place of hurt and fear, and he'd become defensive. What had they said? What had they even been fighting about? She scrambled, trying to piece it together, but it wouldn't come. What she did recall, with sickening clarity, was saying, "Fine. Then let's get a divorce and be done with it."

"I didn't mean it," she said, her throat closing around the words. "I honestly didn't mean it."

He didn't reply.

"I was hurt, and angry, and I don't even remember what we were fighting about, just that I wanted to get back at you somehow. And then when you didn't try to talk me out of it, I thought that's what you wanted, and . . . I've been so miserable, Jack." Tears slid down her face. She wanted so badly to reach out to him, not just touch him but get inside his mind and heart and make him see how terrible she felt, how sorry she was. How could she possibly make this right?

"But why did you even say it? That's not something you just throw out there any time you get angry, Molly. That's emotionally manipulative. Divorce is serious. I thought *you* were serious."

She wiped her cheeks with her hands. "I'm sorry, Jack. You know how I am—I fly off the handle and say things I don't mean. I'm too impetuous, and thoughtless, and selfish . . ."

Suddenly Jack was on the floor in front of her, kneeling and taking her hands in his. "So you don't want a divorce?"

"No. I never did. I love you."

He slid his arms around her and pulled her close, holding her against his chest. She started to sob in earnest. She had missed his arms—his touch—so much, and she clung to him, her heart pounding and yet whole for the first time in weeks.

"I love you, Molly," he said into her hair. "I love you so much—you have no idea. I love your impetuousness, your spontaneity, your energy. I need you. You balance me. And when I thought you didn't want me anymore, I didn't know what to say. It hurt so much."

She cried harder for the pain she'd caused him. After a moment, his shoulders started to shake too, and they held each other tight, mopping up their tears on each other's shoulders.

After several long moments, she pulled back and looked him in the eyes. "So, you really love me?" she asked, just to make sure. She needed to hear it again.

"Like crazy." He wiped the remaining tears from her eyelashes. "Like absolute, total, complete crazy." He took her face between his hands and kissed her, sending a whole family of tingles down her spine. She leaned forward, solidly meeting his lips and breathing in the remnants of his cologne. Now she was sure her heart would break, but this time from happiness.

"Good morning, Agent North," Jack said, taking a seat at the table.

Molly grinned at him over her mug of hot chocolate. "Good morning to you too. How'd you sleep?"

"I have to say, the bed is much nicer than the couch."

She pushed the sack of bagels closer to him, then followed with the cream cheese. "That's what I've been telling you."

They ate for a moment in silence. Molly couldn't stop looking at her husband. His eyes were gorgeous, and his dimples were just adorable, and his muscles were magnificent, and—

"Molly?"

She blinked. "Yeah?"

"Your cell's ringing."

"Oh." She felt her cheeks grow a little warm. "I wasn't really paying attention." She picked up her phone and checked the caller ID. It was Ryan.

"Hi, this is Sarah," she answered.

"Hi. Um, listen. I need to talk to you," he said. There was a slight tremor in his voice, and Molly's danger radar instantly went off.

"Sure, Ryan, not a problem. Do you want to come in a little early? I can meet you at the shop at nine."

"Um . . . okay. That would be great. Thanks, Sarah."

He hung up, and Molly closed her phone. "That was weird."

"What was?"

"Ryan wants to meet me at the shop. Says he needs to talk to me about something important."

"Just you?"

"He didn't say." She picked up her bagel, but then set it down again. "Let's talk this out. You and I both feel that Ryan's not our killer, but I keep coming back to those drugs in the wall. They got there somehow, and the only person who could have put them there had access to the shop. Ryan had keys until we changed the locks. Agent Blevins called Esther, and she said no one else had keys. If Ryan didn't put the drugs there, who did, and is Ryan capable of killing someone?"

"You know as well as I do that people can *become* capable of things."

"True, but that happens only with great provocation. You don't just wake up one morning suddenly ready to go kill someone—unless you're mentally unstable."

"Well, Ryan does play World of Warcraft," Jack said. "He just might be a little unstable."

"Hey, you have to be nice to me. I'm your wife." Molly grinned at Jack, then stood, walked around the table, and wrapped her arms around him. "I'm your wife," she whispered.

"Yes, you are." He pulled her closer and kissed her until she forgot what they'd even been talking about.

"Let's go," Jack said a moment later. "We've got twenty minutes until nine. We'll let him think you're alone and see what he has to say, but I'll crank up the mike in the shop and record everything, and I'll sit backup in the wedding consultation area." He drew his gun, checked it, then slid it back in the holster.

"Sounds good." Molly checked her guns as well, noting that they were fully loaded. She felt a little sick inside. How had a young kid like Ryan gotten himself trapped in this? She knew what it was like to feel desperate—she'd grown up in poverty and had wanted nothing more than to create a real life and solid career for herself where she'd never have to worry about money again. Would she have turned to selling drugs? She honestly didn't know. And is that what Ryan had done? She didn't know that, either.

Jack punched in the security code on the back door of the shop and they entered. Molly paused near the doorway, half expecting—although it was crazy—to smell gunpowder like she had before. There was nothing. No movement, no scents lingering in the air except for the aroma of flowers. She shook her head, realizing how silly she was being.

"I'll go tweak the sound system," Jack said. "Be back in a second."

Molly glanced at the clock—it was almost nine. She should get busy. Giving Ryan a sense of normalcy would help him say whatever it was he needed to say.

She pulled out a bucket of roses and was removing thorns from the first when Jack came up the stairs. "We're set." He took the stool nearest her and reached for a rose and knife. "It'll start recording when I hit the remote, which I'll do as soon as Ryan gets here."

"Thanks." Molly watched as Jack moved the blade down the length of the stem, slicing off the thorns and extra leaves before placing the rose back in the bucket. He made it look so easy. Even with all Tansy's tutorials, it still took Molly twenty seconds to clean one rose—and yes, she had been timing herself.

They worked together in silence, Jack pausing every few minutes to wink at her. She loved the happiness that simmered inside her whenever he caught her eye.

Two buckets of roses later, he shook his head. "I don't think he's coming."

"But he said he wanted to meet." Molly turned and looked at the clock. It was nine thirty. "Maybe he decided to come at ten after all."

"Maybe, but I wouldn't count on it. I'll go by his house."

Molly bit the inside of her lip. "If he wanted to come, but couldn't . . ."

"Yeah. We need to find out what's going on, just to be sure." Jack picked up the first bucket of roses. "Is Tansy coming in today?"

"Yes, at eleven."

"Great. I noticed we were getting low on arrangements." Jack put the bucket in the cooler, then grabbed his keys and headed out.

Molly spent the next half hour tidying up the counter, putting more quarters in the till, polishing the glass doors on the cooler, and getting ready to open. Ryan might have forgotten, or maybe he was sidetracked by something. It could be something as simple as another raid in World of Warcraft. She knew all too well how time flew while one was playing. She talked to herself this way until Jack returned, a furrow in his brow.

"Ryan's mother said he left at a quarter to nine and she hasn't seen him since. I drove around for a bit, looking for him. Nothing."

Molly sighed and pushed a strand of hair behind her ear. "I was hoping we'd get the case wrapped up today."

"Me too." Jack looked at his watch, then grabbed the broom. The floor wasn't dirty, but he liked to clean when he was agitated. Molly guessed it soothed him or something. "If he doesn't show up soon, we'll need to put the word out."

"Give him what, half an hour?"

"Yeah. I asked his mother to call us when he comes home—I let her think it's a minor work-related thing so she wouldn't worry."

"Are we worrying too much? All we know is that he wanted to talk to me, but didn't show up when we thought he would."

"And he's currently the main suspect in a murder case."

"Yeah, and that." Molly fingered the grip of her gun. Jack could sweep to relieve tension—she wanted to shoot something. That wasn't something she could do without arousing suspicion.

The half hour passed and Jack made the call. Blevins relayed the message to the local police, and they agreed to begin a search.

"Agent Blevins said they'll check the bus station and all the other routes out of town, including keeping an eye out for hitchhikers. They've got uniforms going door-to-door starting in his neighborhood and working outward. They should have covered a pretty-good-sized portion of the town by now. And Braden's flying out too."

"He is? For a missing kid?"

"For a missing murder suspect," Jack reminded her.

"How does a boy that tall hide so well in a town this tiny?" Molly muttered.

An hour later, Jack's cell phone rang. "Uniforms found something," he told Molly after he hung up. "One of Ryan's sneakers, shoved under a bush a few blocks from here. They found it, took it to his mom to ID on a hunch, and it's definitely his."

"No." Molly turned and kicked at the garbage can. She missed and her foot collided with nothing but air. It was strangely symbolic of this whole case—a lot of effort, no results. "Nobody goes for a walk and just decides to take off one of their shoes and leave it behind. He was kidnapped." And again, there wasn't much of anything they could do—nothing that wouldn't blow their cover. Right now, in that moment, Molly wished it didn't matter. She'd rather be out there rescuing Ryan than bringing down the mob. He was just a kid, and obviously not their murderer.

Time came to close the shop, and they went home starving and restless. Jack busied himself by making dinner, and Molly paced up and down in the living room. She must have been annoying Jack or something because after a few minutes, he wiped his hands, came over to her, and wrapped his arms around her waist.

"Molly, it's all right. He'll be found and we'll figure out what's going on."

She nestled into Jack's shoulder, loving the feel of his breath on her neck. "I know. I just want to know what's taking so long."

He lifted her chin and kissed her, then stepped away. "If I don't get this in the oven now, we won't eat until midnight."

"I would very much like to eat before then." Molly took a seat at the counter and snitched one of the pepper strips Jack had sliced.

Darkness had fallen early, the brisk autumn breeze picking up outside. Molly turned up the furnace, then mixed some hot chocolate. Melissa was going to have to answer for this new obsession she had. "I hate waiting," Molly said with a growl. "And I hate letting the locals do all the footwork."

"They'll do their job." Jack reached out and ran his fingers through her hair. "And while we wait, I can flirt with my beautiful wife."

"Okay. I like that plan." Molly had every intention of flirting back, but just then Jack's cell phone rang. He put it on speaker as he answered it.

"I'm at the shop and I need backup. One armed suspect." Braden sounded tense.

"Coming." Jack sprinted for the door—pausing to turn off the oven, of course, because he'd never dream of leaving the oven on while he went to apprehend a criminal. Molly was right behind him as he climbed into the car.

It was only two blocks from the house to the shop, but Molly still wished they could flip on a siren and speed through the streets. She'd been in that situation before—alone on the end of a standoff and waiting for backup, with every second feeling like an hour. She wanted to be there for Braden. Although, why was he at the shop? Wouldn't he have come to the house first? It was after business hours. She shrugged. Maybe he thought they'd be waiting for him in the command center.

Once Jack parked the car behind the floral shop, he and Molly quickly got out, closing the doors softly so as not to alert the intruder. The sky was pitch black, and the streetlight did little to break up the darkness. Jack and Molly tightened the straps on their bulletproof vests and then held their guns at the ready as they edged into the shop, placing their feet carefully so they wouldn't be heard. As they rounded the corner into the workroom, they saw Braden in shooting stance, a bulletproof vest strapped firmly around his torso as well. He'd come prepared, thank goodness. Another few steps inside revealed that his gun was aimed at Ryan's chest. Ryan also held a gun, but his hands were shaking and he looked pale, even in the dim light.

Molly instinctively pointed her gun at Ryan too, kicking herself for believing in the boy's innocence. The shoe had obviously been planted, meant to throw them off guard. She'd let her emotions get in the way of the case—something she'd been trained not to do—and she'd been misled.

"Glad you guys are here," Braden said. "Our suspect's in custody—let's get him cuffed."

Molly took a step forward, ready to assist, but paused. Jack hadn't moved, and he was no longer aiming at Ryan. Instead, he had shifted his aim to Braden.

"Drop your gun, Agent King." Jack's voice was hard, resolute.

Braden chuckled. "What are you talking about? Cuff this kid and let's get out of here."

"I said stand down."

Molly looked back and forth between Jack and Braden. She had absolutely no idea what was going on. She'd come down here with every intention of backing Braden up—locating Ryan was icing on the cake—but Jack wasn't paying the teenager any attention.

"Braden King, you are under arrest for the murder of John Ferguson and for possession and distribution of illegal narcotics. You have the right to remain silent." Jack marched through the rest of the Miranda rights while Molly's jaw dropped a little farther with each sentence. A look of incredulity passed across Braden's face as well, and then he burst into laughter.

"Oh, come on." He shook his head. "How long have you guys known me? How many cases have we worked together? You can't be serious." He met Molly's eyes, his gaze pleading with her for understanding. "Really. You can't be."

Molly shook her head slowly, a million thoughts racing through her mind, and then she brought her gun into position. "You've been read your rights. Drop your weapon."

Braden glanced back and forth between her and Jack, looking as though he wanted to say something more. But he didn't. Instead, he sighed, then squatted to place his gun on the floor. Molly glanced at Ryan, who had backed up against the workroom wall—ironically, the same one where the drug cache had been found.

A flicker of movement brought her attention back to Braden. Instead of putting his gun on the floor, he brought it up from his crouched position and fired. Jack threw himself in front of Molly, becoming a blur as he tackled her. The groan he let out told her that he'd been injured, but she couldn't tell how badly. The impact with the concrete floor knocked the breath out of her and she lay there panting as Braden raced for the door of the shop. He was getting away, and Molly wasn't about to let that happen.

She arched her back and brought her gun into firing position. Braden's bulletproof vest made a kill shot difficult, but then he raised his arm to open the door. Molly took advantage of that split second and fired, sending the bullet into his armpit while it was partially unprotected. Another shot sounded from the other side of the room.

Braden slumped to the ground in the doorway, thrown to the side from the impact of the bullet.

"Did— did I do that?" Ryan asked, his voice cracking. He lowered the gun he'd just shot, and Molly had to give him some credit for trying. They'd probably be digging that bullet out of the ceiling.

"No, I did." As Molly lowered her arm and rested it on the cold floor, she felt a sharp tingle in her left thigh. "Is everyone all right?"

"Um, we should be asking you that," Ryan said.

"Well, aside from being pushed to the floor by a really good-looking man and getting my leg all banged up in the process . . ."

"I didn't hurt your leg, Molly." Jack sat up and clutched his arm. "The bullet did. It went through me and into you."

She looked down at her thigh. Blood spilled from her wound onto the floor where she lay. Funny—she hadn't realized she was hurt until that moment, and then she blacked out.

TWENTY-THREE

Before Molly even opened her eyes, she knew where she was by the smell. She hated the smell of hospitals. She groaned, wondering how long she'd be laid up this time.

"Molly? Are you okay?"

It was Jack's voice, more welcome to her than water on a hot day. She smiled and opened her eyes. "Hey, handsome. What's going on?"

"Well, you were shot in the leg."

"I remember that part . . . sort of." She turned her head farther and saw that Jack's arm was in a sling. "How are you?"

He shrugged. "Not bad. Minor surgery to repair some ligaments, and I won't be able to shoot for a few weeks. But you're better at that than I am, anyway."

"Where's Braden?" It was a little hard to talk. Molly's throat was dry, and her tongue weighed about a pound.

"He's recovering down the hall, under tight guard."

"I'm glad I didn't kill him. He was . . . Braden."

Jack didn't reply, but nodded. He always understood what she was trying to say. Well, almost always. There was that whole "Let's get a divorce" fiasco, but she'd decided not to dwell on it.

"You don't look so good."

Jack ran a hand through his hair. "I've been better, I have to tell you. Waiting for you to come out of surgery—it was awful. I was even second-guessing my choice of careers. Should I have been a firefighter instead?"

"You would have been a very sexy firefighter."

Jack leaned over and kissed her, then sat on the edge of the bed and laced his fingers through hers. "Molly, I'm so glad we made up when we did. If you hadn't backed me up when I arrested Braden . . . I hate to think what could have happened. Even a second's hesitation on your part . . ."

Molly shook her head. "Making up had nothing to do with it, Jack. I trust you. I would have backed you up even if we were still getting a divorce."

He smiled, making his dimples appear. "And that's why you're the perfect partner. Thank you."

"I have to ask—how did you know it was Braden?"

"I didn't until we got to the shop and I saw him standing there with Ryan. Then it just hit me. Braden was the only one who could have tampered with the security footage. He was out here last year—he could easily have made connections in the drug world then. The gun Ryan was holding was the gun from Braden's ankle holster—and no way could Ryan have just grabbed it. Braden gave it to him to make him look guilty."

"How did you know it was Braden's gun?" Molly asked.

"I was with him when he bought it. It has a pretty distinctive handle, with ivory inlay. Not from an actual elephant, though—imitation."

"I'll turn you into a gun expert yet."

"Yes, you will." Jack grinned. "But not for about three weeks. I'm not even supposed to brush my teeth with this hand."

"I'm glad, because brushing your teeth with your hand is just gross."

"You know what I mean."

She reached out to touch his face and felt stubble on his cheek. That was odd—he hated having stubble. "How long have we been here?"

"About two days. It's Wednesday night now."

"Really? I missed lunch with the mobster ladies." Molly struggled to sit up, but she got woozy and fell against the pillows, gasping.

"You can't do that," Jack told her.

"Yeah, I just figured that out." She grimaced until the room stopped spinning. "So, how long am I in for this time?"

"About a week, they're guessing."

"A week? A whole week?"

"Molly . . ." He glanced away, and then back. "Molly, you almost died on the operating table. They're not going to send you home without making sure you're all right."

"I did?"

"You did. That bullet ripped your femoral artery to shreds, and you nearly bled to death." He gave her fingers a squeeze. "Thank you for coming back to me."

Molly heard a quiet cough in the doorway, and Jack turned around. George and Ida Mae peeked in from the hall. "Is she awake?"

"She is. Come on in." Jack got up and pulled a few chairs closer to the bed. Ida Mae took one but George refused the other, choosing to stand next to Jack instead.

"Now, just what is going on?" Ida Mae asked. "I understand you decided to have a little adventure in the floral shop."

"Well, you know how it is," Molly said. "I've always got to be in some kind of trouble or another."

"The police are saying that an armed gunman broke in and you shot him in self-defense." Ida Mae leaned forward. "Is that true?"

"Mostly." Molly tried to shift on her pillows, but decided that was a mistake.

"It's what we're letting everyone believe for now," Jack added. "We haven't finished what we came here to do, and we don't want anything getting in the way of our investigation."

Ida Mae nodded sagely. "I see. Well, you're quite the hero in our neighborhood."

"She's definitely *my* hero." Jack grinned down at Molly, and she winked at him.

Ida Mae raised an eyebrow. "So, are things—"

Molly smiled. "Yes, everything is wonderful."

"I knew it. I just knew that if the two of you had a chance to clear the air . . ."

"You were so helpful. Really, you were. Thank you." Molly reached out and clasped Ida Mae's hand. "In so many ways."

"And we don't want you to worry about the shop," George said. "Tansy and Arlette have been running it, and doing a beautiful job, too. Arlette took a look at your books and nearly fainted, so she's been setting up a new accounting system. Tansy's in seventh heaven, and they don't want you to worry about a thing."

"To be honest, I wasn't even thinking about the shop, but I'm glad *they* were." Jack chuckled. "It's probably in better hands than it's ever been."

George and Ida Mae visited with them for a few more minutes, and then an orderly came in, pushing a meal cart. "Are you hungry?" he asked.

"I'm starving," Molly answered, not really looking at him until he set her tray in front of her. Then she smiled. His name tag read "Harold," but she knew better.

"How are you, Mrs. Bennett?" he asked with a wink.

"I'm just fine, thank you," she replied. She knew Special Agent Blevins enjoyed going undercover, but she'd never seen him with so much hair.

"And you must be the incomparable Ida Mae Gilmore," Blevins said, turning to face Molly's visitors. "It's a pleasure to meet you. I'm the Bennetts' supervisor. You've been very helpful."

"Well, I don't know if I'd say I was incomparable," Ida Mae said, her cheeks turning a shade of pink that matched the collar of her blouse.

"I would." George put his arm around his wife's shoulders and squeezed. Molly wondered if she and Jack would be that cute together a hundred and fifty years down the road.

"Aren't you sweet?" Ida Mae kissed George's cheek. "But we'd better go. I'm sure they have a lot to talk about in regards to their case." She whispered the last word.

George led the way to the door, but Ida Mae turned back. "I almost forgot. I brought you something." She fished in her bag and brought out her notebook. "I wrote down everything we've learned so far. I thought you might like this—give you something to do while you're recovering. And there are lots of blank pages in the back so you can make a game plan for when you get out."

Molly was speechless. How did Ida Mae know that her brain was already trying to fill in the missing pieces? "Thank you," Molly managed at last. This was the most thoughtful gift she'd ever received.

Agent Blevins waited to speak until after the Gilmores left. Then he turned back to Molly. "You gave us quite the scare, Agent North."

"Unintentional, I assure you, sir."

He nodded. "I want to thank you for your fine work on this case. The way everything played out . . . well, it was quite a shock to realize Braden wasn't the man I thought he was."

"What happened, sir? How did Braden get involved?"

Agent Blevins took the chair Ida Mae had left vacant. "I was with him just now in his room. He's in pain, but he's talking. He knows he's in a lot of trouble, and he seems willing to tell us everything—well, almost everything. There are still some aspects to the case he won't discuss. I have to say, Agent North, that was some mighty fine shooting, going around the vest like that."

"Strangely enough, being on the floor gave me an advantage." Molly paused. "Help me out here, sir—what happened?"

"When Braden was sent here a year ago, he met up with one of the more influential drug dealers in the state and quickly gained his trust. His assignment had been to make contact with the Mafia, but he realized this was his chance to break away from the agency like he'd planned to do for a long time. His cover was working as a driver for the floral wholesaler, and Esther often had him do odd jobs when he stopped in with her orders. She paid him in cookies. One of those jobs was to fix a loose brick in the wall, and he realized he had a hiding spot for his inventory. He broke into the shop late one night—she didn't have a security system or anything—did a little handyman stuff, and created a cubbyhole."

"He was hiding drugs under Esther's nose the whole time?" Molly asked.

"Yes. He'd come in with her delivery, take out or tuck away what he needed while she was checking the packing slip or whatever, and she was never the wiser. He had an accomplice who also had access to the shop, and they worked together to provide the good people of Omni with all the cocaine they needed."

"Not Ryan," Molly said. "Please say it wasn't Ryan."

"It wasn't. It was Ryan's girlfriend, Heidi."

Molly tried to sit up again, forgetting in her surprise what a bad idea that was. "Braden was Heidi's drug dealer?"

"That's right. She'd been getting her drugs from somewhere else before he came to town, but after he realized what a sweet setup he had, he convinced her to start buying from him. Then she started selling too, and he became her supplier. He realized she could hit markets he couldn't—the teenage crowd and so forth. Over time, she became a partner. Heidi would come into the shop, wait until Esther was distracted, and take the drugs she'd ordered from the wall. It became a very lucrative business for both Heidi and Braden."

"So why were there still drugs in the wall?" Molly asked.

"Braden was called back to HQ and reassigned, and Esther rather suddenly decided to sell the shop not long after that. She locked up before Heidi had a chance to come clean out the wall. When we got this break in the Scarlotti investigation, Braden saw his chance to take care of some loose ends. He's the one who suggested we buy this shop. He thought he could get in here, clean out the drugs, and no one would be the wiser. But when he arrived to help with the setup, agents were swarming all over the place and he never had a minute alone. They were working round the clock, so he couldn't come back after hours. Finally, he decided he'd just wait until all the remodeling was done.

"He was planning on a nice, quiet retrieval at his own leisure, but when you ran that shelving unit into the wall, you messed up his whole plan. Not only would a repairman see that there were drugs in the wall, but he'd see how carefully the hiding spot had been crafted and concealed. It wasn't just a loose brick—it was actually a little door behind a plaster façade, hidden by the roughness of the surrounding bricks.

"So Braden decided to take care of John Ferguson and set Ryan up for the whole thing. Ryan was just handy—there wasn't anything personal in that decision. Except that perhaps Braden could get rid of the problem of Heidi as well, saying that Ryan and Heidi had been working together."

"Wow." Molly thought that over while she rose up on one elbow—very, very carefully—and took a sip of water. "What about all the issues with the security system?"

"Braden patched everything from the shop into his own computer. He had the phone tapped, and that's how he knew John would be in here doing repairs. He could basically manipulate the entire store from anywhere in the world. He made the screens go fuzzy during the murder and then erased every trace that he'd tampered with the security." Agent Blevins shook his head. "We trained him to be one of the best there is, and then he used his knowledge against us. He's been flying back and forth between Utah and California, living a double life, making you think he was in California, and making me think he was working from home or on location with his other assignments.

"He withheld evidence, interrupted the transfer of information, deleted files, tampered with data . . ." Agent Blevins sighed, and Molly could see the pressure this was putting on him. "It may take us a very long time to figure out the cumulative damage that agent has caused. The level of trust we placed in him—this has shaken the very underpinnings of our branch of the agency."

"I don't understand something, sir," Jack said. He'd been quiet, nodding as Agent Blevins spoke, and Molly assumed he'd been filled in while she snored her head off for the last two days. So unfair. "Why would Braden sacrifice so much to run a two-bit drug-dealing ring in a tiny Utah town? He can't possibly have thought it was worth it."

Agent Blevins fiddled with his hospital ID tag for a moment. "You've just hit on one of the most complex aspects of this case. Braden has been forthcoming with almost everything we've asked him, but he's not telling us the entire story. Apparently this was part of something much, much bigger—something that is worthwhile to him—but he won't tell us what or how it's connected. Maybe he'll change his mind after some time in lockdown, but right now, all snug in his hospital bed, he refuses."

"So this was all one piece of a master plan." Jack shook his head. "Braden's one of the smartest men I know. His plan is a doozy, whatever it is—otherwise he wouldn't risk it."

"Do you think we're talking international, or terrorist, or what?" Molly asked.

"We haven't had time to come up with a hypothesis yet. We still need to figure out to what extent he was able to tap into our top-secret files. Our computer guys are on that right now. I imagine a lot of our time will be spent on damage control for the next little while. Then, hopefully, we'll get a full picture. We'll take it as it comes."

"Is our cover blown with the local police, sir?" Molly asked.

"They know who you are now, which will make things easier in some ways and more complicated in others. But as far as the community goes, you're still Jason and Sarah Bennett."

"And the fact that I had a gun . . ."

"It's not illegal for a civilian to carry a concealed weapon in a floral shop," Agent Blevins said with another wink.

They talked for a few more minutes, and then Agent Blevins motioned toward Molly's food tray. "You said you were starving. Eat."

"Oh, that's right." She had been so wrapped up in the story, and so angry at Braden, that she'd forgotten. She took a big swallow of her soup, wishing it was steak, then asked, "Why couldn't we find Ryan all day on Monday?"

Agent Blevins grinned. "I wondered when you were going to ask that. It's a rather interesting part of the case. But I'll let Ryan tell you himself—he's been waiting around for you to wake up." He pulled out his cell phone and made a call. "Send Ryan in, please."

Molly bit into her Popsicle and found it not terrible. Maybe this post-op liquid diet wouldn't kill her after all. When Ryan entered the room, her eyes instantly went to the bandages on his wrists. "Hey, Ryan," she said. "Please come sit down and tell me everything. I've got a million questions, and I want them all answered before I fall asleep. We need to hurry because I'm really starting to get tired."

"We can save this for later," Jack said, but Molly held up her hand.

"Tell me everything now. I'll sleep better."

"Well, so, I was coming to see you at the shop, right?" Ryan began.

"Right."

"I was on my way there, and I was walking past the alley at the end of Main Street. Next thing I know, I'm waking up in a dark closet, with my hands tied behind my back, and my head's killing me. I didn't know what time it was or anything. I felt doped, like I'd been given knockout drops or something. Finally, Heidi's drug dealer, the one I gave the money to last week, came in and got me. I was locked in that closet all day and could barely walk because my legs had been so cramped up. And I was pretty dizzy and nauseated."

"Where were you held? Do you know?" Jack asked.

"It was Tanner's Tires—you know, the place that's all boarded up right now while they paint and stuff?"

Jack nodded.

"No one was in the building," Ryan explained. "I guess they were letting the paint dry or something—the fumes were really strong. Anyway, the guy took me to the shop and called you. Once he heard you coming, he cut the rope on my wrists and pushed a gun into my hands. I was still really groggy from whatever he'd given me, and I couldn't think straight. I couldn't figure out how to run or anything. Then you came in, and you know the rest."

"What did you want to tell us on Monday morning?" Jack asked.

"I wanted to tell you I thought Heidi had been dealing. I didn't want to say anything before because I thought she was getting help, and I love her. I've loved her for a long time, even before we started dating. But too many things didn't add up. And then I started running into her friends on the street and they were asking where she was—not like they wondered how rehab was going, but like they had to talk to her in a hurry. I realized she'd been dealing to them, and you told me I should tell you if I thought of anything." Ryan's eyes flicked back and forth between Jack and Molly. "So, you're not really normal people, are you? I mean, you're normal, but . . ."

Molly glanced at Agent Blevins, and he nodded his permission.

"Ryan, we're undercover FBI agents."

"Really? That's so cool!" He didn't show even a flicker of doubt as to Molly's claim—she guessed that after all he'd seen, he was ready for the bizarre truth.

"We're here to investigate another crime, and the murder sidetracked us for a little while," she explained. "But we'll be in town until we've completed our original task, and we need to ask you for your total secrecy. No telling anyone about us, all right?"

Ryan nodded. "I won't tell anyone, I promise." He paused for a second. "So, did you ever find out who brought Heidi the drugs in the rehab center?"

"We're pretty sure it was Braden, but we don't know how," Jack said. "Everyone who enters the building is searched, so however he did it, he was very creative."

"And that's the first thing I'm writing in Ida Mae's notebook," Molly said, opening the cover. "This to-do list is going to get pretty long by the time I'm released—I can tell that already."

"That guy's really messed up, isn't he? I mean, selling drugs to teenagers, getting Heidi to sell, kidnapping me, shooting both of you . . ."

"He's done a lot of bad things, Ryan, and we're going to try to convict him of all of them," Jack said. "Have you given your statement about the kidnapping?"

"Yeah, I did that yesterday."

"Good. That will be very helpful."

"So, you're still going to work for us at the shop, right?" Molly asked. "I probably won't be able to do much for a little while, and I could use some extra help. Not to mention that Jason's wing has been clipped."

Ryan's eyes grew a little wider. "You still want me? Yeah, I'd love to help out." He hesitated a moment, fiddling with the zipper on his hoodie. "And maybe I could help with some of the arrangements. I wasn't going to say anything, but now that I know you're undercover and you're not really a florist, well, you're not very good."

Molly laughed, then winced as the pain grabbed her leg. "I know I'm not, Ryan, and I'd be more than happy for whatever help you can give me."

He grinned. "Cool."

Jack sat on the edge of Molly's bed, and she held her arms out to him. "Come here," she invited. He kicked off his shoes and lay down next to her very carefully, positioning his arm so as not to bump it. "I don't want to squish you," he said.

"You won't."

They lay there for several minutes, enjoying the quiet moment alone—well, quiet except for the beeping of the monitors near the head of the bed. "You know what I want to do?" Molly asked.

"What?"

"Well, first I want to get out of the hospital."

"That sounds good."

"And then I want to go out to dinner with my ridiculously handsome husband. Maybe take a romantic trip somewhere, just the two of us, with no bad guys and no shootouts."

"That sounds really good."

"And then I want to figure out what Braden's hiding. I can't believe he tricked us for so long, making us think we were friends when all the time, he was concocting this . . . this . . . whatever it is. And then I want to bring down the Mafia."

Jack leaned up on his elbow and planted a kiss square on her mouth. "Those, Agent North, are some of the best ideas you've had in a long, long time."

ABOUT THE AUTHOR

Tristi Pinkston now has twenty-five books published in a wide variety of genres, but that doesn't mean she's slowing down—her love of writing is as strong as ever. She is the mother of four amazing children, the wife of one fantastic husband, and the taker of very, very long naps. When she's not writing or editing, she enjoys watching good movies, and she admits a certain fascination with shows like *Project Runway* and *Dancing with the Stars.* She also enjoys scrapbooking, but finds she doesn't have as much time to do that as she'd like.

Tristi sits on the board of directors of iWriteNetwork. She also works as a freelance editor and author mentor, and she is a regular presenter at writers conferences up and down the Wasatch Front. You can learn more about Tristi and her books by visiting her website at www.tristipinkston.com and her blog at www.tristipinkston.blogspot.com.

Secret Sisters

Ida Mae Babbitt, president of the Omni 2nd Ward Relief Society, didn't mean to become a spy. But when visiting teaching stats are low and she learns that one family under her care is in financial trouble, she'll do whatever it takes to make sure they have what they need. If that includes planting surveillance cameras in their home and watching them from a parked car in the woods, well, isn't that what any caring Relief Society president would do?

With the help of her counselors Arlette and Tansy, Ida Mae soon learns there's more to the situation than meets the eye. It's all in a day's work for the Relief Society.

Dearly Departed

Ida Mae Babbitt has done her community service and is a reformed woman—no more law-breaking for her. But when Arlette's granddaughter Eden discovers a mystery in a fancy nursing home, Ida Mae—with the perfect excuse of a broken wrist and a broken ankle—checks herself into the place. After all, it is for the greater good. Soon she's buzzing around in her motorized wheelchair, questioning the residents and stealing files from the office. She's bound and determined to get to the bottom of this case. But can she solve the mystery before she becomes the next victim?

Hang 'Em High

When Ida Mae Babbitt receives an invitation to visit her son Keith's dude ranch in Montana, she's excited to mend their broken relationship, but not so excited about spending time with cows. Arlette and Tansy go along with her, ready to take a vacation that does not involve dead bodies or mysteries of any sort—one must have a break from time to time. But it seems a no-good scoundrel has moseyed into Dodge City and is bent on causing trouble for the ranch. Unable to keep her curiosity in check, Ida Mae decides to investigate. Can she lasso the varmint and get him to the sheriff in time?

Targets in Ties

After two long years, Ren's mission is over, and it's time for Ida Mae, Arlette, and Tansy to travel to Mexico to pick him up. Their itinerary is all planned out: visit the ruins in the Yucatan, shop, play in the sand and surf, then head to Ren's mission home to be reunited with that dear boy. But a wanted antiquities thief crosses their path, and soon the ladies are tangled in a web of lies, intrigue, and costly jewelry. Held hostage by men desperate for riches, they do what only they can to keep their heads about them, plan their escape, and discuss the proper making of tortillas. Will the Secret Sisters survive their most harrowing adventure yet?

Till Death Do Us Part

When charming—and mostly bald—widower George Gilmore asked Ida Mae Babbitt to marry him, she was surprised and delighted. But now he has made another proposal—to hold the wedding in two weeks, while all his children are in town. Flustered but sure she can handle it with the help of her friends, Ida Mae agrees.

The plan doesn't go over so well with George's family, however, and Ida Made finds herself the victim of a plot to stop the wedding. At first the incidents seem like harmless pranks, but they escalate until Ida Mae finds herself in real danger—and in real pain. Bells are ringing, but are they wedding bells or death knells?